PRAISE FOR

Arguing

with the

Storm

"Editor Rhea Tregebov gets full marks for following up on the ingenious idea of her mother . . . who leads a Yiddish reading circle or *leyenkrayze* . . . [to translate] their favourite stories by Yiddish women writers into English."

—The Toronto Globe and Mail

"Provides an invaluable glimpse into the work of a talented group of writers who have been largely overlooked . . . a surprising diversity of themes is represented. . . . Family plays a central role, especially the challenging relationships between parents and adult children. . . . These female Yiddish authors explore the transition and incongruity between the Old World and the New, often exemplified in the vast divide which springs up between older parents and their modern, American-born children."

—Canadian Woman Studies

"There is a great variety in the material in this book. The stories describe the experience of both women and men in all stages of life, from infancy to old age, in many countries of Europe, including Russia, Poland, Latvia, and Ukraine. There are also stories about Jewish life in both Canada and the United States, as well as Israel."

—The Outlook

"The stories are of suffering and laughter, intolerance and love . . . an interesting aspect is how hard these women had to fight to be writers and authors, considered in the past as being in the male's domain."
— *The Prime Times*

"Vivid. Sometimes shocking. The 14 stories in this collection . . . [are] always deeply moving."
— *The Jewish Post & News*

"The literary careers of these nine writers vary as widely as their origins and geographical migrations. . . . The stories themselves, concise and exacting, reveal unsettling views of the lives of Jewish women, children, and men, in Europe, in North America, and in Israel. Several stories address the ways children survive and grow in hardship."
—from the Introduction by Kathryn Hellerstein, The Ruth Meltzer Senior Lecturer in Yiddish and Jewish Studies, University of Pennsylvania

Arguing with the Storm

❦

STORIES BY

YIDDISH

WOMEN

WRITERS

The Reuben/Rifkin Jewish Women Writers Series
A joint project of the Hadassah-Brandeis Institute
and The Feminist Press

The Reuben/Rifkin Jewish Women Writers Series, established in 2006 by Elaine Reuben, honors her parents, Albert G. and Sara I. Reuben. It remembers her grandparents, Susie Green and Harry Reuben, Bessie Goldberg and David Rifkin, known to their parents by Yiddish names, and recalls family on several continents, many of whose names and particular stories are now lost. Literary works in this series, embodying and connecting varieties of Jewish experiences, will speak for them, as well, in the years to come.

Founded in 1997, the Hadassah-Brandeis Institute (HBI), whose generous grants also sponsor this series, develops fresh ways of thinking about Jews and gender worldwide by producing and promoting scholarly research and artistic projects. Brandeis professors Shulamit Reinharz and Sylvia Barack Fishman are the founding director and codirector, respectively, of HBI.

Arguing with the Storm

ॐ

STORIES BY

YIDDISH

WOMEN

WRITERS

EDITED AND WITH A PREFACE BY RHEA TREGEBOV
INTRODUCTION BY KATHRYN HELLERSTEIN

The Feminist Press
at the City University of New York
New York

Published in 2008 by The Feminist Press at the City University of New York
The Graduate Center, Suite 5406, 365 Fifth Avenue, New York, NY 10016
www.feministpress.org

Copyright © 2007 by Rhea Tregebov
Introduction copyright © 2007 by Kathryn Hellerstein
Page 169 constitutes a continuation of this copyright page.

Originally published under the same title in Canada by Sumach Press in 2007.

Library of Congress Cataloging-in-Publication Data

Arguing with the storm : stories by Yiddish women writers / edited by Rhea Tregebov.—1st Feminist Press ed.
    p. cm.
Includes bibliographical references.
ISBN-13: 978-1-55861-558-8 (pbk.)
ISBN-10: 1-55861-558-X (pbk.)
ISBN-13: 978-1-55861-559-5 (library)
ISBN-10: 1-55861-559-8 (library)
    1. Short stories, Yiddish—Women authors—Translations into English. 2. Yiddish fiction—20th century—Translations into English. 3. Yiddish literature—Canada—Translations into English. I. Tregebov, Rhea, 1953-
PJ5191.E8A74 2007b
839'.1301089287—dc22

2007021441

Printed in Canada

13 12 10 09 08   5 4 3 2 1

Contents

❧

For Jeanette,
with such gratitude

Preface and Acknowledgments

❦

Arguing with the Storm, the title of this anthology, comes from the poem "My Home" [*mayn heym*] by Yiddish poet Rachel (Rochl) Korn. Korn writes about her young widowed mother who "divided her years between her fields/ and her three children" (Korn 1976, 91–92). She dreams of full harvests, but black hail clouds threaten to "trample the world." When the storm threatens:

> *then she would hide us in a corner*
> *far away from the lightning in the windows, chimneys, and doors,*
> *and we could hear her voice arguing with the storm*

Although the poem was published before the Second World War, the impending storm can be seen as a metaphor prefiguring the Holocaust and the destruction from which so few were successfully hidden. The mother's defiance remains a paradigm of courage and resistance, and an appropriate emblem for the fourteen stories in this volume.

Arguing with the Storm contributes to the renaissance of Yiddish literature, a movement which gained momentum in 1980 with the establishment of the National Yiddish Book Center in Amherst, Massachusetts. The significance of the Center's recovery of 1.5 million volumes of Yiddish books for a new generation of readers cannot be underestimated. In *Outwitting History* (2004), Aaron Lansky, founder and now president of the Center, describes how, as a graduate student in his early twenties, he rescued Yiddish books that were decaying in cellars and being disposed of in dumpsters.

Arguing with the Storm would not exist were it not for the talent, commitment, persistence, and energy of the Winnipeg Women's Yiddish Reading Circle from which it arose, along with the dedication of the Circle's volunteer coordinator, Jeanette Block. The Reading Circle was established in 2000 by a group of seniors whose Yiddish skills varied, but whose interest in writing by women had been piqued by their involvement with the Winnipeg Jewish Public Library, which had a large and significant Yiddish collection. Inspired and tantalized by the quantity and quality of the titles by women they had discovered in the library's collection, the group felt frustrated that these works were largely unfamiliar, and that the literary achievements of their writers had been lost.

The reading circle, or *leyenkrayz*, is a long-standing platform for literary discussion. In the Winnipeg Women's Yiddish Reading Circle a reader adept in Yiddish reads aloud to the group. This format allows individuals of varying linguistic ability or literacy to participate. As the readings and the Reading Circle expanded, some members began independently to translate the stories. I encountered the stories first through translations brought to my attention by Jeanette Block, who is my mother. My own Yiddish is minimal, but I was immediately struck by the power of the voices in translation. As I learned more about the authors and their stories, I suggested that an anthology of translations be compiled for publication. Since an earlier, landmark translation of stories by Yiddish women writers, *Found Treasures* (Forman et al. 1994), had served as a starting point for the Reading Circle, I was also convinced that a new anthology would serve as a means of introducing other Yiddishist groups to these women's writings.

Selection of the stories was a lively and engaging process in which the group discussed and evaluated the stories and then passed on the translations of a few for me to read. We were all committed to an inclusive vision that would embrace the wit, humor, satire, and compassion of *yiddishkayt* (Yiddish culture), as well as its tragedy. For those stories to be included, we began a painstaking, but also joyous process of translating and editing. I am extremely grateful for the skill, wisdom, and patience of the Winnipeg Yiddish Women's Reading Circle translators—Luba Cates, Esther Leven, Arnice Pollock, and Roz Usiskin. I want to express a particular appreciation to Esther Leven, whose translation skills are evident in five of our fourteen stories. Our fifth Winnipeg translator, Chana Thau, is a member of a younger reading circle called (tongue-in-cheek) the Next Generation, and it was her expertise in translation and Hebrew, as well as in Yiddish, that made possible the translation of Rikuda Potash's stories. Goldie Morgentaler, daughter and translator of Chava Rosenfarb, the only living Yiddish writer included in the anthology, was gracious in offering us one of her translations. No anthology of translations from the Yiddish would be complete without representation from Chava Rosenfarb, whose status as a national literary treasure is unquestioned. As the project progressed and expanded, we were delighted to include translators Miriam Beckerman, who translated Paula Frankel-Zaltzman's Holocaust memoir, and Professor Sacvan Bercovitch, who with his sister Sylvia Ary translated their mother Bryna Bercovitch's memoir.

One of our greatest hopes is that the anthology will provide a springboard for other Yiddish reading circles. To this end, we have included a brief bibliography of works in Yiddish. Although Yiddish is strongly related grammatically to German, it is written in the Hebrew alphabet. Thus any transcription involves a transliteration from Hebrew to Latin (English) characters. Since variations in transliteration of the authors' names alone present many difficulties for those seeking out the original texts, we wanted to ensure that these were available in Yiddish.

The decision about how much Yiddish to leave in the translations rested intimately on the goal of reaching as broad an audience as possible. To make the book as accessible as possible to non-expert readers, we have minimized the use of Yiddish words in the text except where they are necessary to carry a concept or cultural value, or where the English equivalent carries the wrong connotation, as, for example, in the use of "bastard" for "*mamzer.*" Wherever an anglicization exists for a Yiddish word, we have used it: "cheder" instead of "*kheder*," for example. For Yiddish words that have no English or anglicized equivalent, and for the book and story titles, we have used the YIVO (*Yidisher visnshaftlekher institut*; Yiddish Scientific Institute) standardized transcription system. For proper nouns used for characters in the stories, we use anglicized spellings for ease of reading for non-expert readers: using the more familiar Chana, for example, rather than Khane, and spelling the diminutive "le" as "leh" (Chanaleh not Khanele) so that the final "e" is pronounced.

ACKNOWLEDGMENTS

Many thanks to The Feminist Press for taking on the American publication of this book with such enthusiasm and commitment. My deepest gratitude to the women at Sumach Press, my Canadian publisher, whose encouragement from the earliest stages gave me the incentive to undertake this project. A special thanks to Jennifer Day of Sumach Press for her superb eye in editing.

For their patient and generous assistance with the Yiddish translations, thanks to Menorah Waldman, Edith Kimelman, and the entire Women's Yiddish Reading Circle, Winnipeg. We'd also like to thank Evelyn Shapiro, Frieda Forman, and Osher Kraut.

Thanks to the following individuals for their kind assistance in the research for this anthology: Carla Elm Clement; Janet Gould and staff at the Kaufman-Silverberg Resource Center, Winnipeg; Eddie Stone, Library Technician, Jewish Public Library, Montréal; Mervin Butovsky, Concordia University; Yael Chaver, University of California at Berkeley; Leonard Prager, University of Haifa; Sonia Silva, Humanities and Social Sciences Library (McLennan-

Redpath), McGill University; Kimberley Hintz, Librarian, Humanities & Social Sciences Division, Koerner Library, University of British Columbia; Lynda Yankaskas, Historian for the Jewish Women's Archive; Yeshaya Metal, Reference Librarian, YIVO Institute; Wendy Lee; Abby Yochelson, Reference Specialist/English Literature, Humanities & Social Sciences Division, Library of Congress; Mary Mark Ockerbloom, Celebration of Women Writers; Jill Rosenshield, Associate Curator, Department of Special Collections, Memorial Library, Madison, WI; Seth Jerchower, Public Services Librarian, Center for Advanced Judaic Studies Library, University of Pennsylvania; Donna Becker MacDermot, Program Coordinator, Peretz Center for Secular Jewish Culture, Vancouver.

I gratefully acknowledge the University of British Columbia for supporting research for this project with a SSHRC-HSS Large Grant from the UBC Internal Grant Program.

Rhea Tregebov
Vancouver, British Columbia
November 2007

WORK CITED

Forman, Frieda, Ethel Raicus, Sarah Silberstein Swartz, Margie Wolfe, editors. 1994. *Found Treasures: Stories by Yiddish Women Writers*. Toronto: Second Story Press.

Korn, Rachel. 1976. "My Home." In *Canadian Yiddish Writings*, edited by Abraham Boyarsky and Lazar Sarna; translated by Seymour Levitan. Montreal: Harvest House.

Lansky, Aaron. 2004. *Outwitting History: The Amazing Adventure of a Man Who Rescued a Million Yiddish Books*. Chapel Hill, N.C.: Algonquin Books.

Introduction

The nine authors gathered in this anthology of Yiddish short fiction and memoir, *Arguing with the Storm*, would probably not have said in so many words, or even known, that they were writing within an old tradition of women. Nonetheless, the presentation of these distinct and varied writers together in one volume and the selection of narratives with common themes, characters, and conflicts make a good case for arguing that there is a tradition of women prose writers in Yiddish.

Women began writing stories in Yiddish, the thousand-year-old vernacular language of Jews in Europe, long before the idea of a modern Jewish literature arose. Most of these stories were set within devotional texts—prayers or collections of moral fables—and the identities of the authors were often ambiguous. The most famous of these early writers, Glikl bas Reb Leyb Pinkerle, widely but incorrectly known as Glikl of Hamel, wrote her memoirs in Yiddish between 1691 and 1719 (Davis 1995, 8–9; Turniansky 2006, *tet*, 309 note 397).[1] Glikl intended her work to be a kind of ethical will and moral treatise for her children and grandchildren, to instruct them how to live a good Jewish life and to remind them of their family heritage. Within this didactic, religious framework, Glikl proved to be a master storyteller.

Along with an account of her life as a daughter, wife, and

mother, Glikl's book included moral parables, folk tales, gossip, accounts of historical events, descriptions of matchmaking, weddings, and funerals, interpretations of Jewish law and custom, and an account of the international jewel business, in which she, her first husband, and some of their twelve children worked. Glikl's book also contained at least one narrative that today we would call a murder mystery, the story of Frau Rebecca, the energetic wife of Reb Lipmann of Hamburg, who, thanks to her insomnia and her penchant for looking out of windows, uncovered the murderers of two Jewish money changers and averted a violent uprising against the Jews (Lowenthal 1977, 184–197). Glikl's memoirs, while entertaining her readers with such gripping stories, also illuminate the dark corridor of history in which Jewish women passed their lives, off the record of the official accounts of Jewish history in Europe.

Professor Chava Turniansky, the editor of the definitive Yiddish text of Glikl's writings and their Hebrew translator, notes that, from these stories, we can learn how girls were educated in the Jewish languages of Hebrew and Yiddish as well as in the gentile languages of French and German, how their parents married them off, how women traveled throughout Europe as merchants and matchmakers, and how Jewish families were scattered geographically, yet confined by the laws and decrees of governments and churches (Turniansky 2006). That the personal narrative of one woman could be a rich source for cultural history is relevant to *Arguing with the Storm*.

Most of the writers in *Arguing with the Storm* had probably not read Glikl's memoirs, which remained in manuscript for almost two centuries after she had composed them. Only in 1896 was the book first brought into print in Glikl's archaic Yiddish. In the 1910s, two German translations were published, and two English translations in 1932 and 1962. A partial modern Yiddish translation came out in a Warsaw newspaper in 1922, and a full translation in Buenos Aires in 1967. The scholarly edition of the old Yiddish text with a modern Hebrew translation appeared in Israel only in 2006 (Davis 1995, 215–216; Mosley 2006, 156–157; Turniansky 2006, *nun-gimel–nun-zion*).

Despite the inaccessibility of Glikl's memoirs, the authors in *Arguing with the Storm* owe their ability to express their lives in prose to the development of Jewish autobiography. As the European Enlightenment began to improve the political status of Jews in Western Europe at the end of the eighteenth century, the Jewish Enlightenment, or *Haskalah*, emerged first in Germany and later in Poland and the area of Russia in which Jews were permitted to live, known as the Pale of Settlement. The *Haskalah* implanted the notion that Jews could be citizens of nations, an idea that led to a secularization of Jewish life and to Jewish writings that would not primarily serve religious law and devotion. Modeling their books on Jean Jacques Rousseau's *Confessions*, early-nineteenth-century Jewish men began to write accounts of their own lives and educations in Hebrew, German, and Yiddish in order to teach the future generations "the follies of their predecessors" (Mosley 2006, 335, 333–376). These works revealed the struggle between the traditional Judaism of their origins and the enlightened ideas that drew them into the world.

In 1864, the young *maskil* Sh. Abramovitsh discovered that his satires of traditional Jewish life could best reach the common people he sought to instruct in the vernacular language of Yiddish, rather than in Hebrew, the sacred language that acquired a high literary register in early secular writings. To deflect the "disgrace" of writing in what was considered the lowly mother tongue, or *mame-loshn*, he took on the pseudonym Mendele Moykhr Sforim (Mendele the Bookseller), and wrote novels considered the first works of modern Yiddish literature (Miron 1973, 16–17; Seidman 1997, 47–53). Later in the century, when Abramovitsh and other enlightened Jews observed that modernization would diminish and ultimately erase the traditional Jewish world, their satirical and autobiographical works came to preserve ethnographically the culture from which they had escaped (Seidman 1997, 57–66; Mosely 2006, 454).

Under the influence of the *Haskalah*, a few exceptionally educated women wrote journalism, fiction, or memoirs, as well as translations, poems, and letters, in Hebrew, Russian, and German. In the 1870s and 1880s, Miriam Markel-Mosessohn translated works on Jewish history from German into Hebrew and wrote articles for *Ha-melitz*, a Hebrew newspaper in Russia (Balin 2000, 32–33, 40–41). In the 1880s and 1890s, Rashel' Mironovna Khin wrote short stories and novellas in Russian (Balin 2000, 93–98). Sarah Feige Meinkin Foner published the first Hebrew novel by a woman in Vilna, in 1881, and Hava Shapiro wrote the first manifesto calling for women to write literature in Hebrew, in Warsaw, 1909 (Zierler 2004, 29–34).

By 1900, as modern Yiddish literature matured in the writings of I. L. Peretz and Sh. Rabinovitsh (known by his pseudonym as Sholem Aleichem), and through their publishing activities, women began tentatively to publish fiction in Yiddish. Paradoxically, the authority with which Peretz and Sholem Aleichem infused literary endeavors in *mame-loshn* made Yiddish, once scorned as the "women's language," a territory in which women writers themselves were not fully welcome (Klepfisz 1994, 40, in Forman et al. 1994; Seidman 1997). In Russia, Dvora Baron, daughter of a rabbi in Ouzda, published short stories as a young girl first in Hebrew in 1902 and then in Yiddish in 1904; as an adult, living in Israel, however, she published only in Hebrew (Seidman 1997, 68, 73). In Warsaw, Yente Serdatzky published her first story in 1905 in *Der veg*, encouraged by its literary editor I. L. Peretz, and, after she immigrated, her work appeared in the New York Yiddish newspapers from 1907 through 1962. Prolific as she was, Serdatzky was lucky to publish her only book of short stories in 1913 (Forman 1994, 365–366). Fradl Shtok, a poet and fiction writer from Poland, was also fortunate to have her collection of short stories appear in New York in 1919. But after her book received negative reviews by male critics in the Yiddish press, Shtok published a novel in English and then fell silent. Esther Singer Kreitman, the older sister of her famous writer-brothers, Israel

Joshua Singer and Isaac Bashevis Singer, published two novels and a collection of short stories in Yiddish during the 1930s. From 1942 through 1974, the poet Kadya Molodowsky published two novels, a collection of short stories, several plays, a volume of essays, and a serialized autobiography, in addition to seven books of poetry.

Despite the fact that throughout the twentieth century more than a hundred women published prose in Yiddish, scholars and translators did not begin to collect, translate, teach, or study their works until the 1990s, after feminist scholarship had come to the fore (Norich 2006). As Irena Klepfisz writes in her Introduction to *Found Treasures*, a 1994 collection of Yiddish stories by women, which, as Rhea Tregebov tells us in her Preface, inspired *Arguing with the Storm*, the women writers of the early twentieth century found themselves in a paradoxical situation: caught between the gendered strictures of an observant life they had left and the "unfulfilled promises of secular liberation" (Klepfisz 1994, 51, in Forman et al. 1994). Indeed, they were caught between arranged marriages, enforced modesty, and childbearing, on the one hand, and, on the other, the unrealized ideals of women's equality and self-determination. Klepfisz points out that the women who published stories seemed to be writing in an echo chamber, unlike Sh. Rabinovitsh's Tevye, the pious dairyman. He complains about his rebellious daughters to Mr. Sholem Aleichem, the authorial character within the fiction who, Tevye presumes, will convey his stories to an audience who will understand the dilemmas of Jews caught between tradition and modernity. In stark contrast, the women narrators or protagonists in stories by Rochel Brokhes, Sarah Hamer-Jacklyn, and Chava Rosenfarb seem to be talking to themselves or trapped in their own silence (Klepfisz 1994, 54–55, in Forman et al. 1994).

Arguing with the Storm grows out of the groundbreaking effort to establish women Yiddish narrative writers, begun in *Found Treasures*. Like the earlier anthology, *Arguing with the Storm* took shape initially as a communal project among the Winnipeg Women's Yiddish Reading Circle (see Tregebov's Preface to this collection). That an informal group of women took on the task of translating and selecting works, which editor Rhea Tregebov has brought into print, is itself a phenomenon in tune with the writers and stories in this volume.

Extending the chronological range of *Found Treasures*, *Arguing with the Storm* collects stories and excerpted memoirs composed and published in the second half of the century, from 1940 through the 1990s. Like the earlier anthology, *Arguing with the Storm* includes works that appeared originally in Europe, Israel, and the United States, but it also includes works published in Canada. It is no coincidence that five of the nine writers settled in Canada, where this anthology's editor and translators live. It is worth noting, though, that Winnipeg lies a great distance west of Toronto, where Sarah Hamer-Jacklyn settled, and even farther from Montreal, the home of Bryna Bercovitch, Paula Frankel-Zaltzman, Anne Viderman, and Chava Rosenfarb. Of these five Canadian Yiddish authors, Bercovitch, Viderman, and Hamer-Jacklyn arrived in Canada from Russian Turkestan, the Ukraine, and Poland respectively, before World War II. Frankel-Zaltzman, who survived the Dvinsk and Riga ghettos in Latvia and the Shtuthof concentration camp, and Rosenfarb, who survived the Lodz ghetto and Auschwitz and was liberated from Bergen-Belsen, left Europe as displaced persons for Canada after the war.

Two of the anthology's writers came to the United States. Frume Halpern, born in 1888,[2] came to New York in 1905, the year after Malka Lee was born in East Galicia; Lee immigrated to New York in 1921. Rikuda Potash, born in Poland in 1906, is the only writer in the anthology who went to Palestine, where she settled in Jerusalem in 1934. And Rochel Broches, the oldest of the writers, born in 1880, lived in Minsk her whole life, and perished in the Minsk ghetto in 1942.

The literary careers of these nine writers vary as widely as their origins and geographical migrations. From age 20, Sarah Hamer-

Jacklyn published stories in Yiddish newspapers and periodicals across North America (Canada, New York, Mexico), and in three collections of her writings (1946, 1954, and 1964). Bryna Bercovitch came to writing much later in life, after a brutal career as a political activist in Russia, as a columnist for the Montreal Yiddish newspaper, *Der kanader adler* (The Canadian Eagle) from 1945–1956. Her writings—mostly autobiographical or topical—were never published in book form. Paula Frankel-Zaltzman composed the memoir of her experiences during the war while she lived in Fernwald, the displaced persons camp outside of Munich, and published it privately in Montreal in 1949. Anne Viderman, like Bercovitch, was a columnist for *Der kanader adler*, but she was able to collect and publish two volumes of her columns, stories, and memoirs in 1946 and 1960. In contrast, Chava Rosenfarb has been consistently a prominent literary figure, from when she was a very young poet in the Lodz ghetto and the DP camp in Belgium, until the present day, when she is best known for her epic novels about life in Poland before the war and life in the Lodz ghetto. Her short stories and novellas appeared in the foremost literary journals in Canada, the United States, and Israel; they and her five novels have been translated into English, and she has received prizes and other honors for her writing.

The New York writers are equally diverse. Unlike Bercovitch and Viderman in Montreal, Frume Halpern was never a columnist for the newspaper, though she did publish her short stories there, in a literary quarterly, and in anthologies. As such, she reached an audience. Her work of four decades was salvaged from the oblivion accorded most journalism by a group of colleagues who published one volume of her collected writings when she was 75 years old. In contrast, Malka Lee was an ambitious and visible figure on the New York Yiddish literary scene, from her debut in 1922 and her first book of poetry in 1932, through her 1954 memoir and her 1966 book of children's stories.

Like Rosenfarb and Lee, Rikuda Potash was recognized as a poet from her 1924 debut book in Lodz through the numerous collections of plays, novellas, short stories, and poems she published in Israel. Rochel Broches, too, was a significant presence in the literary journals of Minsk, Warsaw, and Vilna, from her first published story in 1899, through her plays and the collections of her work that appeared in 1922, 1937, 1939, and 1940. She was considered important enough to have a retrospective edition of her more than 200 short stories prepared by the State Publishing House of White Russia, although it was lost when the Germans invaded the USSR in 1941.

Despite the diverse lives and careers of these nine writers, this anthology presents evidence for the development of a tradition for women prose writers in Yiddish. Moreover, by placing journalism, memoir, and belles-lettres on equal footing, *Arguing with the Storm* challenges a linear historiography of literature as well as the conventional hierarchies of writing.

The stories themselves, concise and exacting, reveal unsettling views of the lives of Jewish women, children, and men, in Europe, in North America, and in Israel. Several stories address the ways children survive and grow in hardship. Both Sarah Hamer-Jacklyn's "No More Rabbi!" and Anne Viderman's "A Fiddle" are narrated in the first person by a woman who recalls her girlhood relationship to a male cousin. In "No More Rabbi!" the narrator tells how she, as a shtetl girl, transgressed her beloved aunt's rules of kosher purity by letting her famished baby boy cousin nurse at the breast of a gentile. The girl narrating "The Fiddle," recounts the decline and death of her beloved cousin Motya, a soldier discharged from the Russian army, whose brilliant fiddle playing cannot redeem him but inspires her. In both these pieces, the girl narrator feels mystified by the behavior of the adults around her, at the same time that her empathy for her cousin brings out her generosity and imagination.

Malka Lee's "The Apple of Her Eye" and Rochel Broches' "Little Abrahams" both come to us through an omniscient narrator whose point of view shifts from that of a woman responsible for the care of a very young boy to that of the boy himself. In "The Apple of Her Eye," the mother of the newborn "Sonny" does her best to feed and clothe him and his siblings in a basement hovel in immigrant New York. A widow, she must work long hours, and so leaves the baby in the care of his six-year-old sister, herself sickly and hungry. Malnourished, unattended, ever in the basement's dank twilight, the baby cannot thrive. Yet when the mother brings home a cheap print of a landscape under a blue sky, the now three-year-old Sonny, inspired by the artistic image of daylight, gets to his feet and walks.

There is no art to redeem the boy Avremeleh in Broches' "Little Abrahams." This story, perhaps the most disturbing and brilliant in the collection, tells how an old, childless woman, Baba Bryna, earns her pittance in a shtetl by caring for the *mamzeyrim*—babies abandoned by their adulterous mothers, who, Broches suggests, may also be prostitutes. The boys are all given the name "Avremeleh" (the diminutive of "Abraham") by the shtetl shammes, and sent to Baba Bryna's hovel by the cemetery, where she keeps them, starving, in a kind of stable, for use by "legitimate" nursing mothers who need to relieve their engorged or infected breasts. The illegitimate girl babies are left, nameless, to die. Eventually, the boys, too, die. They starve to death, having sucked dry the "sugar soothers"—chewed bread wrapped in a dirty rag. Or the desperate Bryna feeds them to the hungry dog outside the window. Or, if they survive to the age of two, and grow too many teeth to be useful at a woman's breast, Bryna abandons them in a strange neighborhood.

This is what happens to Avremeleh, whose point of view the narrator enters, when he eats the bread from the other babies' pacifiers, when he nurses delightedly but all too briefly at the breasts of two new mothers—one legitimate and the other not. The cleverness of this curly-haired child, "not yet two," and his ability to articulate what he wants, sees, and comes to know, and even Bryna's rough-handed, reluctant affection for him cannot save him. The shtetl itself is as guilty as Bryna for reducing this human being to "dust, dirt, nothing." In the world of poverty and harsh religious law, the old childless spinster, Baba Bryna, and the young women who give birth—both the proper wives and those who have no husband—are also "dust, dirt, nothing." Broches' short story is an excoriating criticism of that culture.

Other stories in the anthology challenge societal mores that demean people—women, men, children, Jews. Bryna Bercovitch, in "Becoming Revolutionary," reflects on how she, as a young girl, joined the revolutionary party and then army in Russia, to overthrow the political injustice that framed and forced Jewish poverty. Bercovitch depicts her family, and especially her mother in this hard life with affection, and reveals the brutality of the Revolution and the betrayal of its aftermath.

In contrast to the European stories, Sarah Hamer-Jacklyn's "A Guest" looks at the Americanized son and daughter-in-law of the widowed Dvora-Zisel. They insist that she live with them, but deprive her of a relationship with their baby. In the United States, however, this old woman can create meaning for her own life by working in a factory and living on her own. Frume Halpern also criticizes middle-class and wealthy Americanized Jews. In "Blessed Hands," Halpern depicts Sarah, "an independent individual" who has made her way in the world as a masseuse with gifted hands. Less generous than she would like with her talents to the poor and the sick, Sarah must cater to the spoiled, wealthy women who can pay. In "Goodbye, Honey," Halpern criticizes corrupted female empowerment when Molly, a still-youngish widow who has supported herself and raised her sons through the beauty parlor business she has built, retires to marry an old, rich man she despises. In her luxury, she learns to abuse the African American maid. Hamer-Jacklyn's "A Love Story" provides a more gentle critique of the sexual politics between women and men. In an old age home, the widowed Malkaleh meets her former fiancé from the shtetl, rumors of whose non-pious ways had spurred her parents to cancel the wedding when they were young. Now that they can choose, they fall in love again. When a doyenne of the Yiddish theater appears, he has to win Malkaleh's confidence in his commitment to her.

The two stories of the Holocaust in this anthology bring us back to the theme of children and parents. Paula Frankel-Zaltzman's "A Natural Death" tells how, in the terrible conditions of the Dvinsk ghetto in 1941, she nursed her father through his final illness and watched him die. Caring for her father, when she had lost the rest of her family, provided the young Frankel-Zaltzman with a purpose to her life in an environment of extreme hunger and deprivation. His "natural death," celebrated by others in the ghetto as better than dying at the hands of the Nazis, leaves the narrator empty and bereft, but perhaps, tragically, better able to survive.

Chava Rosenfarb's dramatic monologue, "Letters to God," perhaps the most developed and sophisticated work in the anthology, also reflects upon how the suffering of Jews during the war subverts the relationship between child and parent. The narrator, a psychiatrist, Dr. Yacov Sapir, survived a concentration camp with his father as a boy and, now years later, keeps his dying father in a room closed off from the rest of the house. Rosenfarb depicts the story's main woman character as extremely unsympathetic. Malka, Yacov's wife, urges her husband to administer stronger and stronger injections of morphine, because she is aesthetically offended by the dying man's presence. Yacov writes letters to God, whom he calls, "Great Absent One." The son, who had saved his father in the camps, also addresses his "*Tateshe*" (Daddy) and recalls his childhood with the man whom he both despises and loves. Yacov hates his father because he had resumed his revolutionary idealism after the war, while discouraging Yacov from following his own ideals to become a poet. In ironic revelation, the frustrated artist rages against his own creators, the father he had rescued and God. When he kills his father, Yacov thinks of himself not as a Jew who takes leave of another Jew, "with the blessing, 'Be well, go in good health, come back in good health.'" Instead, identifying with the Nazi murderers, he calls himself "your son Cain, I, your murderer who loves you," and foresees how his own little son Sammy will someday betray him. As in many of her other works, Rosenfarb examines the complexity of power and loss of agency among Jews who survived the concentration camps, within the fraught relationships of children and parents, and within the narrator of the story, who struggles to articulate the contradictions of human experience against the silence.

Ultimately, the stories in this anthology argue against the diminishing of women's lives and the silencing of women's voices. When, in Rikuda Potash's "Rumiya and the Shofar," the tiny Mizrahi washerwoman laughs at the Jerusalem matron's insult, she assumes the grand lineage of the matriarchs Mother Sarah and Mother Rachel, asking, "Am I not of the same family?" And she imagines that she might give voice to the fundamental sound of Jewish triumph by blowing the shofar that belonged to her late husband, even though the pious Jerusalem that Rumiya inhabits forbids this Jewish voice to women.

Which brings me to the title of this anthology. As Rhea Tregebov writes in the Preface, she has taken the title, "Arguing with the Storm," from a poem by Rachel Korn, a prominent Yiddish poet and fiction writer from Poland, who survived the war in the Soviet Union and wrote in Canada from 1948 until her death in 1982. In Korn's poem, a widowed mother protects her young children from the raging weather by articulating her fears, her anger, and her strength. Likewise, the short stories and memoirs in this book give voice to rage and beauty, as storytelling has for the centuries in which women, denied the shofar, have written in Yiddish.

Kathryn Hellerstein
Philadelphia, Pennsylvania
November 2007

NOTE

1. The page numbers to Turniansky's Introduction are in Hebrew letters, which have been transliterated in this Introduction.

2. Frume Halpern's birthplace is unknown.

WORKS CITED

Balin, Carole B. 2000. *To Reveal Our Hearts: Jewish Women Writers in Tsarist Russia*. Cincinnati: Hebrew Union College Press.

Davis, Natalie Zemon. 1995. "Arguing with God: Glikl bas Judah Leib." In *Women on the Margins: Three Seventeenth-Century Lives*. Cambridge, Massachusetts: Harvard University Press.

Forman, Frieda, Ethel Raicus, Sarah Silberstein Swartz, Margie Wolfe, editors. 1994. *Found Treasures: Stories by Yiddish Women Writers*. Toronto: Second Story Press.

Klepfisz, Irena. 1994. "Queens of Contradiction: A Feminist Introduction to Yiddish Women Writers." In *Found Treasures: Stories by Yiddish Women Writers*, edited by Frieda Forman, Ethel Raicus, Sarah Silberstein Swartz, Margie Wolfe. Toronto: Second Story Press.

Lowenthal, Marvin, translator. 1977. *The Memoirs of Glückel of Hameln*. New York: Schocken Books.

Miron, Dan. 1973. *A Traveler Disguised: The Rise of Modern Yiddish Fiction in the Nineteenth Century*. New York: Schocken Books.

Mosley, Marcus. 2006. *Being for Myself Alone: Origins of Jewish Autobiography*. Stanford: Stanford University Press.

Norich, Anita. 2006. "Yiddish Literature in the United States." In *Jewish Women: A Comprehensive Historical Encyclopedia*, edited by Paula Hyman and Dalia Ofer. Jerusalem: Shalvi Publishing Ltd.

Seidman, Naomi. 1997. *A Marriage Made in Heaven: The Sexual Politics of Hebrew and Yiddish*. Berkeley: University of California Press.

Turniansky, Chava, editor and translator. 2006. *Glikl: zikhroynes 1691–1719* (Glikl: Memoirs 1691–1719) (Yiddish, with Hebrew translation and introduction). Jerusalem: The Hebrew University.

Zierler, Wendy. 2004. *And Rachel Stole the Idols: The Emergence of Modern Hebrew Women's Writing*. Detroit: Wayne State University Press.

Publisher's Note:

In these translations, "America" generally refers to the
United States and Canada.

Sarah Hamer-Jacklyn

❦

Although she emigrated with her family from Poland to Toronto in 1914 at the young age of nine, Sarah Hamer-Jacklyn's writing is rooted in the rich experience of shtetl life. She was born into a traditional Chassidic family in 1905 in Novoradomsk, Poland. After the family had immigrated to Canada, she learned English attending public school in Toronto. Hamer-Jacklyn maintained the connection to her mother tongue both at home and with private tutors, as well as through visits to the local Yiddish theater. In 1921, at the age of sixteen, she began acting and singing with a Yiddish theater troupe that toured across North America. She was married, and had one son. In 1934, Hamer-Jacklyn's first short story, "The Shopgirl," appeared in the Yiddish daily newspaper *Der tog* [The Day]. Further stories appeared in numerous newspaper and literary periodicals across North America, including *Tsukunft* [Future], *Vokhnblat* [Weekly News], *Der kanader adler* [The Canadian Eagle], *Yeg* in Mexico, and *The New Yorker*. Collections of Hamer-Jacklyn's short stories include *Lebns un geshtaltn* [Lives and Portraits], published in 1946, *Shtamen un tsvaygn* [Stumps and Branches] in 1954, and *Shtot un shtetl* [City and Town] in 1964. She died in New York on February 9, 1975, at the age of seventy.

Sarah Hamer-Jacklyn's "No More Rabbi!" *[Oys rebe]* was published in the 1954 short story collection *Shtamen un tsvaygn* [Stumps and Branches]. This comic tale takes place in the Polish shtetl setting with which she was so familiar. Hamer-Jacklyn portrays the mix of superstition and pragmatism that governed family life in the shtetl with wry affection. She also depicts the intricate and tenuous relationship between the Jewish and gentile population. The story also provides an interesting window onto the dynamics of how women of that era managed the contradictory needs of motherhood and enterprise.

"A Guest" *[A gast]*, which she dedicated to her sister Chava, was published in the 1946 short story collection *Lebns un geshtaltn* [Lives and Portraits]. While the story is set in the New World (likely the New York City area in which Hamer-Jacklyn lived) during World War II, it links back to the world of the shtetl from which Hamer-Jacklyn, and its characters, originated. The protagonist, Dvora-Zisel, finds herself initially caught between worlds: unable to conform to the new standards of child-rearing her daughter-in-law adheres to and initially unwilling to relinquish the Old World family bonds that defined her. The economic independence the war economy gave women of that era, however, offers Dvora-Zisel both a new life and a new vision of family.

"A Love Story" *[A libe]* was published in the 1964 short story collection *Shtot un shtetl* [City and Town]. "A Love Story" also delineates the bridge between Old and New Worlds. Many decades after their betrothal was ended by rumor and parental intervention, Malkaleh and her long-lost childhood love, Chatzkeleh, meet in the old folks' home where they are both residents. Although the artistic Chatzkeleh of the Old World has become real-estate broker Harry in the New World, his affection for Malkaleh, as well as his artistic talent, remains. In this compassionate story of mature love, Hamer-Jacklyn demonstrates the delicate dance between desire and propriety Malkaleh must negotiate.

No More Rabbi!

❧

SARAH HAMER-JACKLYN

Translated by Roz Usiskin

My Auntie Chaya and Uncle Isaac's house was my second home. Here, in this overcrowded house of thirteen children, I started to develop a good appetite. My aunt once saw my poor mother running after me offering a piece of buttered white challah and an egg; I ran from her as though they were poison. My aunt boasted that in her home, I would fight for a piece of dark rye bread just like her own children. After that, my mother let me go as often as I wished to my aunt's, even to stay overnight. Often I wouldn't come home until Shabbes was over.

My aunt and uncle's house was one with their shop, a spice store. The house portion was large and held a kitchen as well as a parlor. A curtain divided the space. Beyond the curtain, the mother and father's two wooden beds were piled high with cushions. In the middle of the room, you could always find a crib for the youngest child.

At one side of the house was a long dark windowless room with a row of beds for the children. At night, when my aunt counted the children—not one . . . not two . . . not six . . . not eight . . . not twelve—if she counted an extra child, she knew it was me.

The house was always in an uproar, as if it were market day. There were children and adults, the family, brides and grooms, in-laws, engagement parties, a bris . . . And on top of all this, there were the happy sounds of children, the smell of cooking, a stove filled with pots, and the continual sound of a kettle boiling.

Their oldest daughter, Yentel, was already married and had a little boy only one month older than her own brother. Mother and daughter would often help nurse each other's children. My aunt was of average height with a round figure and smiling brown eyes. Her daughter Yentel was very like her mother, only a bit taller and thinner. My Auntie Chaya was the buyer for the store and often would have to travel to larger cities to buy goods. Often, being a pious woman, she would make a side trip to visit the Rabbi to seek his advice. Then she would stop in Carlsbad, where she enjoyed submersing herself in the Carlsbad mineral and salt waters.

Her greatest dream was to raise at least one of her sons to be a rabbi. That was why she sent her children to the best schools and later to the yeshivas. But as soon as they grew up, they would disperse in various directions: one son got friendly with the Social-ists and talked of revolution; the second went to learn a trade at a clockmaker's. And so Auntie Chaya pinned her hopes on the middle son, Simcha-Bunem. He had a good head on his shoulders, was always engrossed in his studies, and followed his mother and father's advice.

Then one day, the ten-year-old suddenly tucked his prayer curls behind his ears, stuffed his prayer shawl under his pants, rolled up his caftan and went off enthusiastically to play football with the boys on the street. He would come home singing gentile songs. My aunt wept. She realized that her dream had evaporated, that her son would never become a great rabbi. Whenever she would meet a rabbi, she would pray that she would be worthy of raising as devout a man as he.

Auntie Chaya's father died a day after the birth of her youngest child. She wept bitter tears for her father, a great scholar, but was comforted in the knowledge that God had blessed her with a son. This she saw as a sign. They named the child Yochanan, after his grandfather, and my aunt was sure that one who carried the name of the great man would grow up to be a pious scholar, a great rabbi.

She raised the child with a great deal of love and special care. She never called him by his name Yochanan, instead calling him "my scholar," or "my *rebele*," my little rabbi. The entire family used the nickname the Rebele. Whenever she traveled, she left instructions that no wet-nurse was to come near him. No outsiders' milk; only her daughter was allowed to nurse him. If he should happen to sneeze or yawn, she would try to fend off the evil eye by kissing his eyes and spitting three times. Around his neck he wore a red ribbon that had a little bag hanging from it. The bag contained a wolf's tooth as a charm to thwart the evil eye.

So Yochanan lay in his crib with his lucky charm, sucked his little fingers, and screamed. A greedy little thing and a screamer, he had to be constantly quieted either by the breast or with a wet rag wrapped around a piece of sugar. He strongly resembled his father, who placed great importance on his food, just the opposite of his thin and shrunken grandfather, who had fasted more than he ate. I was very attached to the child because he carried my zaida's worthy name. So I rocked him and sang him "Raisins with Almonds."

When the Rebele was eight months old, my Auntie Chaya left for a lengthy trip. As usual, the child was taken to Yentel to nurse. She would do this clandestinely. Her husband, Benjamin, disapproved of the whole idea. It seemed to him that his own frail child was being deprived of its best and only source of nourishment. Benjamin was a merchant who dealt in flax and corn. He always had a pencil tucked behind his ear because he was always figuring, and he figured that the brother would deplete the sister's milk, thereby depriving the nephew. This did not sit well with him.

This became a constant bone of contention between husband

and wife; she continually sought ways to hide the unwanted nursling she loved. Yentel would quietly sneak into her parents' home, sit by the crib and bare the breast which Yochanan would eagerly fasten on and nurse. Then she would quickly run back to her own child. However, for Yochanan, with his plump red cheeks, this kind of nursing was not always satisfactory. He would often begin to cry soon after, demanding more. With loud screams, he would keep pushing away the wet rag wrapped around the sugar.

Four days had gone by already, and Auntie Chaya was still traveling. At the break of dawn, with the first sound of the rooster crowing, Yochanan woke screaming, demanding his due. Their older daughter Adele then began to wake one of the younger children so they would take the baby to Yentel's, but nobody responded to her begging and pleading. They didn't want to crawl out from under their warm quilts. From the long dark bedroom, you could hear their even breathing, their orchestral snoring, whistling and snorting.

I then crawled out of bed and dressed quickly. Without washing, I wrapped myself and the howling Yochanan up in a large shawl, knotted the shawl at the back, and left for Yentel's. It was early summer. A new day was dawning. The sun was rising high in the clear blue sky, casting its golden rays onto the whitewashed, crooked little houses, which still had their shutters closed. The shops were also closed with iron bars.

My childish footsteps echoed along the cobblestones. Yochanan, snuggled at my waist and lightly rocked, stopped his crying. An old Jew with a large beard, carrying his prayer shawl and tefillin, was hurrying to the synagogue. Out of nowhere, a peasant appeared in a wagon filled with fruit. *Giddy-up! Giddy-up!* He cracked the whip that he used to hurry along his scrawny horse, which could barely pull the heavy load.

My cousin Yentel lived some distance from her mother and father's house. I passed the synagogue and followed the footpath that led to her house as well as the cemetery. It was already the fourth day that I had brought the child to nurse. Each time,

Benjamin would meet me with a dark, angry look, a look that was ready to devour both me and the Rebele.

Hard as it was for me to carry the child, it was even harder when Benjamin greeted me with eyes which pierced like needles. I arrived at their whitewashed house earlier than usual. The shutters were still closed. I knocked lightly, but nobody answered. It was quiet, and it seemed that everyone was asleep. I knocked harder, and slowly one half of the shutter opened. Benjamin stuck out his disheveled head and, with half-closed eyes, asked in a quiet angry voice, "What do you want?"

"Yentel to nurse him—" I showed him the child. I couldn't understand the foolish question.

"Go away!" he ordered. "She's tired and sick. She was awake a whole night and just fell asleep!" And he closed the shutter and disappeared.

I was left bewildered, but I soon regained my composure and knocked harder and doggedly shouted, "Open up! Open up! The baby's hungry!"

It was quiet. There was no answer.

"Have pity on your little brother," I pleaded, as Yochanan's howls broke the silence of this quiet, still-sleeping street.

The shutter opened abruptly. Benjamin stuck his head out, glared at me with fiery eyes like sharp knives and hissed through clenched teeth, "Get away, if you don't want me to pour this slop pail over you! I'm warning you!" He reached out, shook his finger at me, banged shut the shutter, and disappeared again.

I was confounded. The child was crying and I didn't know what to do. After thinking it over, I decided not to give up. I would not take home a hungry child. Slowly, I moved closer to the front porch and, as I was about to knock on the door, Benjamin appeared in his long johns carrying a slop pail in his hand. I jumped back instinctively.

"See?" He pointed to the slop pail. "If you don't leave now, I'll pour this over you and the Rebele! . . ."

He lifted the slop pail in the air, ready to douse us.

Frightened, I shielded the child with both hands as I beat a hasty retreat. As I got further away from Benjamin, he yelled, "Go, find a good cow or some healthy *goye!* . . ."

I ran and the crying child was rocked and fell asleep. After a while, I stopped running. This time, Yochanan started to cry in earnest. None of my rocking, cradling, or singing seemed to help any longer. On my way home, carrying the hungry child, I began to think that, God forbid, he might die if he didn't get fed. Who knew when my aunt would come home? What should I do? I was in despair. I kept walking.

The town was beginning to awaken from its night dreams. Flowers were ready to bud. Fresh dew like drops of milk rolled from the green leaves. This was how Mother Earth fed her children. Today, however, Yochanan had no mother and I was carrying him home unfed.

Here and there, a Jewish woman carrying warm baked goods and fresh milk walked by. Jewish men were now returning from prayers. The iron bars were now being removed from the shops. From Bayla's dressmaker shop, Chaim-Moisheh, her husband, hung on the door Bayla's colorful peasant clothes made of cheap cloth. From her store, Kayla, the *zogerin,* the prayer leader for the women in the synagogue, rolled out a barrel of sour pickles, a sample of her salty wares. Each morning, Jewish shopkeepers eagerly awaited their first customer. This was the omen for the start of a good day.

As I came close to the house and went into the courtyard, I could see from afar pockmarked Manka, who was sitting on her father's doorstep breastfeeding her child. The father of her child was unknown, so everyone in town called her "Manka-with-the-bastard." Manka was a tall healthy gentile woman with light blond hair, a short nose, and a pockmarked face. She had small narrow blue eyes that always seemed to be laughing furtively under heavy, light-colored eyebrows. She sat with two full white breasts visible through her unbuttoned blouse. Milk was leaking freely from them like the overflowing udders of a cow.

Her child, whom she called Yanek, clearly resembled his mother. He sat on her lap contented, playing with his little feet and refusing the breast that his mother kept urging upon him. In that moment, I remembered Benjamin's words: "Go find some healthy *goye.*" Suddenly, a thought occurred to me. I went up to her and pointed to Yochanan. "Manka, have pity and nurse a hungry child!"

"Go away. You and your little Jew can go to the Devil!" she said heedlessly as she started to button up her blouse.

"Manka," I begged her, "Have pity on the child! His mother is traveling somewhere and he hasn't nursed in a long time. He'll die of hunger! He'll surely die!" Yochanan looked greedily at the full breasts and suddenly began to howl.

Her maternal feelings aroused, Manka began to soften, and said, "Well, may the cholera take both of you! . . . Give me the little Jew—I'm not short of milk! . . ." She drew him to her breast and the child began to suck with such enthusiasm that the woman began to laugh, crossed herself and called, "Oh, my God, what a greedy little thing! . . ."

His cheeks now red and smeared, Yochanan was finally satisfied. I carried him back to the house, put him into the crib, and he quickly fell asleep. Excited, I ran to the older daughter, Adele, and told her of the adventure that the child and I had experienced that day. Agitated, Adele turned pale, wrung her hands and, in despair, shouted, "What have you done?! . . ." Frightened, I looked at her, wanting to say something. But in that instant, Uncle Isaac ran in, having heard everything through the thin walls. He exploded. "Get out! Get out of my house! Don't show your face here again! Get out!" He opened the door and hustled me out of the house, all the while shouting at me, "Scram! Get going!"

I went home crying, unable to understand the terrible thing that I had done. In my muddled thoughts, I knew that something was not right and this kept churning over and over in my nine-year-old brain. Two days later, when my aunt came home, I stood tearfully under her window, not daring to go into the house. She saw me, came out and, sadly, in a trembling voice, said, "Do you realize what you've done?"

"No." I shrugged. "I don't know."

"Because of you, the Rebele's not kosher any more . . . No more rabbi! —"

And she herself began to weep bitter tears.

$\mathcal{A}$ $\mathcal{G}uest$

✎

SARAH HAMER-JACKLYN

Translated by Esther Leven

With love, a gift to my sister Chava.

$\mathcal{A}$LL WAS QUIET IN THE MILSTEIN HOME. DVORA-ZISEL LAY on the sofa, her eyes closed but her ears open. She was on the alert, ready to jump to her feet at the slightest sound from the baby's crib, should he need tending.

Jenny, her daughter-in-law, had gone to the movies; her son Leon worked nights at a munitions factory. In the evenings, after the son had left for work and the daughter-in-law had gone out with her lady friends to play bridge or to a theater, Dvora-Zisel would be left alone with the child. It was then that she was happy, because for a while, she was the one who was in charge of the house and who had full responsibility for looking after the child— whom she loved with all her heart, as though he were her very own child. She often thought that she fussed over this six-month-old

13

grandchild more than she ever had over her own children.

The child made a sound. Dvora-Zisel jumped up and, swift as a cat, was beside the crib. Sleepily, the child turned his head, making sucking noises. Dvora-Zisel gently shook the crib as she looked nervously towards the door. That was all she needed—for Jenny to come in and see her shaking the crib.

Such strange parenting—she says you must let a child cry, even howl, but leave him alone . . . says it won't hurt him a bit, he'll develop strong lungs.

It's outrageous! How can a mother listen to that and just sit nonchalantly by and read the funnies?

Oy America, America, she sighed.

The child fell asleep and Dvora-Zisel carefully covered him, noting how much he looked like her late husband, and thereby wishing the child many long years.

Zelig, her late husband, had been a wonderful person. The baby should only have his character. A person without gall, they used to say of him, a heart of gold.

Dvora-Zisel went into the foyer where her folding cot was kept, opened it, straightened the bedding on it and went to bed. She turned the light off but kept her ears open.

In the darkness she began to imagine scenes from the past, and that past seemed as vivid as though it were only yesterday. North America disappeared. She pictured herself in Plovna, her old shtetl. Her husband, Zelig Milstein, had been a grain merchant. He had been in charge of a large business and Dvora-Zisel had been in charge of the lavish household which had one maid for the house and another for the children. The two boys not only went to cheder; they had hired tutors for Russian and Polish as well. Her daughter, little Sarah, was small; just three. Dvora-Zisel's home was known throughout the district. They had furnishings of the most stylish sort; the whole family dressed in the finest; nothing was too good for her children. But Dvora-Zisel didn't forget about the poor. She was truly grateful that God had granted her such wealth, and there was always a guest or two at her table. Food would often be sent to the poor families. Anyone who was in need would come to the Milsteins' door knowing that he wouldn't leave empty-handed. Dvora-Zisel was the light of her husband's life. To him she shone like seven suns; he simply worshipped her. However, as it turned out, Dvora-Zisel probably wasn't worthy of so much good fortune.

She could remember it all so clearly. Zelig had caught a cold, but, being a busy man, had paid no attention to his illness. When he finally took to his bed, it was too late. He died within a few days.

So there she was—a widow with three children. She could have remarried, but she wouldn't hear of it. To all her family's advice and urging she had only one answer: *I don't want my children to have a stepfather!*

Her brother in America kept writing to her to come to New York, "because your children's future lies in America."

It was not easy to part with the home where she had spent the best years of her life and to leave for a strange land. She loved every street in her shtetl: the old marketplace, the Saxon garden where she liked to stroll, the bridge over the brook which meandered into the small river where she used to bathe as a young girl. She left all this behind for the "Golden Land," for her children's future.

The hardships she endured were many. The big city of New York swallowed her up. She rushed to the shop, pushed into the subway, left the children in the street . . . and when she came home all worn out, she had to tackle the housework and the cooking.

With help from her brother, she opened a little candy store. Things got a little better, but not easier . . . at least the children didn't have to be on their own in the street. They were the ones who helped her in the business.

She brought her three children up to be fine, kind people, but they all scattered. Her oldest son lived in California; he'd gotten married there but Dvora-Zisel had never even met his wife. All she had were photographs.

When her daughter Sarah got married, Dvora-Zisel sold her

little store and used the money to put on a lovely wedding. The couple made their home in Chicago and were doing very well; they had a three-year-old little girl.

She longed to see that child. They sent more pictures, more poses, but pictures—they were just pictures . . . If they had sent her a ticket and invited her, she would have traveled and seen the little girl in person. *But I know,* Dvora-Zisel thought, *it's America and everyone is busy . . .* She would get to see them some day as long as she stayed healthy. She shouldn't complain.

After Sarah's wedding, Dvora-Zisel stayed in her home with her younger son, Leon, and ran the household. Leon even gave her his paycheck. She managed well and frugally, and put a little aside. When Leon married Jenny, Dvora-Zisel handed him the bank book with $1,200 in savings.

Dvora-Zisel wasn't sorry. She had said to him as plain as could be, "You now have a wife, my son, and you should give *her* your earnings."

And he did. They fixed up a nice home and she stayed with them. But she contributed her share—she cleaned, cooked, baked. When Jenny was pregnant, Dvora-Zisel wouldn't let her bend down for a single thing. She had done everything for Jenny like a devoted mother, and she still did. However, since the child was born, her daughter-in-law had become a different person. Whatever Dvora-Zisel did for the baby didn't please her. Jenny didn't trust her with him. Only when she had to go out did Jenny leave her with him. And it was then that Dvora-Zisel had her greatest pleasure.

Suddenly Dvora-Zisel heard footsteps and the sound of the key turning in the lock. Her daughter-in-law came in. Now Dvora-Zisel could relax and throw off the chains of watchfulness that had kept her bound to the baby's crib.

She fell asleep easily, knowing that the child now had another watching over him, even though, she thought—*not as well as I do . . .*

Dvora-Zisel slept for a while and in her sleep, she heard the child crying. Frightened, she opened her eyes to his loud cries. She got up and ran up to the crib, ready to give it a shake or change the baby's diaper, when she heard her daughter-in-law's voice:

"Please, mother-in-law, go away from the crib and don't shake it." And in a louder voice, Jenny continued, "In America we don't rock children. How many times do I have to tell you that?" Her voice was angry, hard and commanding.

Dvora-Zisel felt as if she had been slapped. True, Jenny had told her many times not to rock the baby, but never in this tone of voice. Dvora-Zisel silently left the room, went back to the foyer and lay down on her cot. But the baby's cries became even louder. This lasted about ten minutes and Dvora-Zisel felt like something was pulling her from her bed. The child *must* want something. Such a tiny one can't say "give me" when it wants something, so it cries. That's how they speak. She hadn't done too badly bringing up her children nice and successful, *keynahore*. She remembered very well that she hadn't left them to cry their little hearts out just like that for no good reason. It wasn't letting her rest, so she swallowed her pride and softly entered her daughter-in-law's bedroom, thinking to excuse her daughter-in-law's behavior. Maybe she was tired, sleepy . . . that's why she had spoken so sharply . . . she didn't really mean it . . .

"Jenny-leh, are you asleep?" she asked quietly.

"No, I'm awake. What is it now?"

"You know . . . I mean . . ." she stammered, "maybe he's hungry?"

"Please, mother-in-law," Jenny spoke angrily, "the baby is on a schedule . . . under a doctor's care, and you know it's not yet the proper time for his bottle. He'll have to wait."

The child was crying so hard that he couldn't catch his breath.

"And how much longer for his schedule?" Dvora-Zisel asked resignedly.

"Another forty minutes."

"*Vey iz mir*," Dvora-Zisel exclaimed, wringing her hands. "Will you let him cry like that for the full forty minutes?"

"Yes," the daughter-in-law answered coldly.

"Even the doctor says that if he cries so hard, you can feed him a little sooner," Dvora-Zisel pleaded.

But at this her daughter-in-law lost patience and told her plainly not to interfere in her affairs . . . it was *her* child and she could do with him what she pleased . . . and she knew better than Dvora-Zisel how to look after a baby. She was not in the old country, where children were brought up like wild animals.

"I didn't bring up wild animals, only fine healthy children." Dvora-Zisel stood her ground. "And I gave them a good—"

"Please," Jenny interrupted, not letting her finish. "I don't want to hear these stories and I especially don't want you to mix in with my child's upbringing and when Leon comes home I'll tell him about this and let it be understood once and for all that *I* am the baby's mother and I have full supervision of my child! *Me!*"

At this she gestured for Dvora-Zisel to leave the room and not bother her anymore.

Dvora-Zisel went out of her daughter-in-law's room to her bed and felt as though the ground were giving way under her feet. She couldn't think straight, but she sensed that no good would come of this incident. She was surprised by the rudeness of the tone of voice that her daughter-in-law had used, even though she had noticed how Jenny was always unhappy when Dvora-Zisel was attending to the baby. Jenny was, on the other hand, always pleased with Dvora-Zisel's housework and liked her cooking, her baking . . .

The child was still crying and Dvora-Zisel felt she couldn't lie still. The baby's cries caused her such pain because they seemed to her to be hunger cries.

The clock showed twenty minutes before six. She comforted herself that Leon would arrive at six o'clock and that he would, as he always did, give the baby a bottle of milk. She was also certain that as soon as Jenny told Leon about the disagreement which had just taken place, he would firmly blame his wife and tell her how wrong she had been.

Suddenly there was silence. The baby was worn out and had fallen asleep.

At six o'clock Leon came home from his night job. He was covered in dirt like an old-country chimneysweep. It pained her to see her son, the accountant, so soiled and grimy. With a college diploma he was building ships! But at the same time she was proud that he was at least a small cog in building the ships that would destroy the enemy.

She heard him go into the kitchen to warm the baby's bottle. She then heard him push the nipple into the sleeping child's mouth, who, half-asleep, started to suck so eagerly that you could hear it all through the house.

Her daughter-in-law meanwhile was telling Leon about the words she had had with his "Ma." Dvora-Zisel couldn't catch it all but she clearly understood that Jenny was telling him about what had happened between them. This didn't bother Dvora-Zisel. On the contrary, she was certain that her son would tell his wife how wrong she had been and would ask her to apologize for such a scathing attack on his mother. She heard them close the door, which had been left open. She closed her eyes and relaxed, thinking that her son would soon straighten it all out.

At four that afternoon, Leon was still asleep. He would be getting up soon, because they ate at five and at six he left for work, where he stayed on the job till the next morning.

Jenny had just come in from outside with the child. She left the baby in the foyer and went into her husband's room.

Dvora-Zisel was busy at the pots in the kitchen, but when she saw the child was alone, she ran up to him, took him in her arms, and made some faces that made the baby laugh. Suddenly the door of the bedroom opened and her son came storming out. Eyes filled with anger, he yelled at her, "Mama, put the baby down! The baby was playing. What do you want with him?"

"When he cries I mustn't go to him and when he is quiet I mustn't either? So when may I?"

"Never! You, Ma—do the housework and let my wife take care

of the child. She is the child's mother and you should let *her* look after him."

"And I? Am I, God forbid, a stepmother? When I am in the house and hear him cry, I run up to him . . ."

"Don't run. Nobody asks you to and he gets more upset. My wife has suffered enough from your small-town ways . . . here, Mama, in America, it's not the old country. Here children are brought up differently; we don't rock them. You, Mama, have spoiled him and my wife can't take any more . . . From today on, I don't want you to mix in with my child's upbringing."

He grabbed the child from her and went back to the bedroom, slamming the door behind him.

Dvora-Zisel was as stunned as if she had been had hit over the head with a club.

*

A few days had gone by since Dvora-Zisel had had words with her son, and the atmosphere in the house was strained: she didn't talk to her daughter-in-law and her son said merely, "Hello, Ma" and "Goodbye, Ma." Dvora-Zisel did not go near the baby at all. She wanted to show them that if that was what they demanded of her, she could comply. In fact, she wanted to show them that she didn't care . . . but how difficult it was for her! Whenever it happened that the child cried hard or lay uncovered, she couldn't resist and would approach the crib to cover him or perhaps change his position. Her daughter-in-law would always appear at her side and utter "never mind" through clenched teeth, which meant "it's not your business." Then, like a whipped child, Dvora-Zisel would retreat and find a corner to cower in.

It continued to grow more tense in the house. Dvora-Zisel decided that she must do something about it.

She had tried to talk to her son—to tell him that she meant no harm when she wanted to help with the child, because she knew how, since she had brought up three children. But he wouldn't even listen. He had only one reply: "Don't mix in. You are *my* mother but not the baby's mother, and if my wife doesn't want you to go near him, it will be as she wishes."

Days and weeks dragged on. Dvora-Zisel felt like she was slowly dying. To be in the house with the child but not be able to come close to him was for her the greatest cruelty. Only when her daughter-in-law had to go out and her son was asleep could she be happy. She would run to the baby when he was playing or had just woken up, and take him in her arms and hold him tightly against her. The child knew her and would laugh or wriggle with pleasure and then she knew the greatest joy. Her ears were always tuned to the door and when she heard her daughter-in-law's footsteps, she would quickly put him back in his crib and run into the kitchen to busy herself with some work.

Dvora-Zisel was lying in her bed but couldn't sleep. The house was quiet. The baby and her daughter-in-law were asleep, but sleep would not come to her. She lay there in the dark planning a way out of her hellish situation. She had to find a way out, a plan, a change . . . something . . . things could not go on this way.

Maybe, it occurred to her, she should go visit her daughter Sarah in Chicago? They say that a daughter is closer to her mother than a son . . . But Dvora-Zisel felt the same towards all three of her children. She loved them all alike. Suddenly Dvora-Zisel made a face; the wrinkles in her forehead seemed to deepen. She pressed her lips tightly together and muttered through clenched teeth, "No, it will not do." She was frightened by her own voice and it seemed to her that in the stillness of the night a strong voice answered her, *No, it will not do.* She burrowed deeper under the blankets and shut her eyes, but sleep eluded her. She now understood better than ever why the thought of living with her daughter disturbed her. Just as *she* was now living with *her* son, there too in Chicago a mother had been living with *her* son—with Dvora-Zisel's son-in-law and her daughter. Reading between the lines of the letters which she had received from her daughter, she had gathered that they hadn't been getting along too well with the old lady . . . but Dvora-Zisel had never given it much thought. When Sarah finally wrote her that she couldn't take it anymore from her mother-in-law, Dvora-Zisel had been certain at that time that her daughter was not at fault. But now she saw the situation in quite another light, and she could deeply sympathize with the old lady who, in her old age, had had to move into an old folks' home and spend her remaining years a stranger among strangers . . . So how could she even consider going to Chicago? But maybe to her son? To Leibel? But she realized immediately that that was out of the question. They had never invited her to come visit them, so how could she go there uninvited?

Suddenly her face lit up. She sat up in bed and clapped her hands. Dvora-Zisel was not even seventy years old, just in her early sixties, and she was able-bodied and could still earn a livelihood. Not so long ago she had been a widow running a household. With her own ten fingers she had managed all her affairs and brought up her three children to be fine people. Surely she would be able to earn enough for her needs, especially now, with a war on. It didn't matter whether you were young or old, as long as you could do a job . . .

With this thought in mind, her eyes became brighter and she suddenly felt she'd become a younger woman.

The clock struck four. Around seven in the morning she would get up and buy a newspaper and find a job. She would show them that she was not too old to be an independent person. She did not have to ask for help from her children. Perhaps then they would have more respect for her.

Her eyes shut and she fell asleep happily, knowing that she had finally found a way out of the unbearable state that she had been living in of late . . .

*

For the past two weeks Dvora-Zisel had been working for Caseman & Company, a munitions manufacturer. She sat at a long table with many women of all ages, and packaged bullets. Dvora-Zisel's job consisted of putting together little containers for bullets. At first she had felt very strange. The whole procedure had seemed difficult. But now she felt like an old hand at it. It no longer felt so tiring. Dvora-Zisel had found another woman her age and they ate lunch together. They would talk about various things, world events, and always ended up talking about old age and its problems. They had tried to guess each other's age and both had reassured the other that they didn't look a day over fifty. The fact that their hair was gray or white didn't mean a thing . . . Dvora-Zisel's friend had a niece who was not yet fifty but she had white hair. So did that mean anything? Nonsense!

"And who today has naturally black hair?" persisted Dvora-Zisel's new friend.

"A person is as old as they feel," Dvora-Zisel philosophized.

"Only a short while ago I felt ten years older than I am and now I feel ten years younger than I am, so I've recently become twenty years younger!"

Dvora-Zisel had a hard time getting used to the fact that she earned twenty dollars a week and had become an independent person. She lived at the home of a former neighbor, Doba, who, like herself, was now a widow. The difference was that Doba's late husband had left her an insurance policy which paid her enough to support herself. Doba hadn't wanted to live with her children and she was quite lonely, so she had been very happy when Dvora-Zisel moved in with her. Dvora-Zisel paid her ten dollars a week for board and room and was very pleased with her new home. They often went out together. On Saturdays they went to the Jewish Theater. Doba got Dvora-Zisel to join her community group and they went to meetings and other activities. Doba, who was very active in community work, got Dvora-Zisel to become active in doing "good works."

You would often see Dvora-Zisel at lunchtime running around with a little book of raffle tickets to sell. She handed them out and took the money, all the while encouraging her donors to "buy more, a blessing on you, it's for poor orphans" or "buy, buy—it's for a poor family." She did this with great compassion. Every time she finished a book, when she went back to her work she felt she had done a good deed. Dvora-Zisel felt as though she had slept away her beautiful summer years and had awakened at the end of fall going into winter. *Autumn is also beautiful . . . even winter has beauty,* she told herself. But she was often lonely for her children, especially her grandson . . .

Leon hadn't wanted her to move out. He had said that he wanted her to stay, but he hadn't asked all that forcefully. Her daughter-in-law had never said a thing about Dvora-Zisel staying with them.

*

It was Sunday, at noon. Dvora-Zisel was riding in the subway on her way to her son's home. She was carrying parcels full of toys that she had bought for the baby. Her heart pounded with apprehension. She hadn't seen them for six weeks. Yesterday she had received a letter from her son and daughter-in-law inviting her to come for lunch on Sunday. She had accepted the invitation with joy.

Dvora-Zisel knocked on the door. Her son opened it, genuinely happy to see his mother. The daughter-in-law greeted her holding the child in her arms.

Dvora-Zisel opened the packages and gave the child the toys she had brought. Her daughter-in-law handed the child over to his grandmother . . .

After the meal, Leon started to ask her about her new lifestyle. How did she spend her time? What did she do? And was it really true that she was working in a factory?

When she told him it was indeed true and she was working and happy, he couldn't stand it, blurting out, "Don't be so foolish—a woman your age should go to work in a factory, and a munitions factory at that! It's a shame and an embarrassment. I won't allow my mother to work . . ."

"What do you mean, you won't allow me to work? What else should I do?"

"I want you to give up your 'job' and come back to live with us . . . and not have to live a lonely life in your old age . . ."

It pleased Dvora-Zisel to hear her son asking her to come home. But for the short period of time that she had been away from the house, a new world had opened up for her. She felt that she too had a life . . . a little late perhaps, but it is never too late to correct a wrong.

"No, my son," Dvora-Zisel answered in a firm voice. "It was a mistake from the beginning that I agreed to live with you, so I would like to correct that mistake. It is true that I am no longer young, but I would like to start anew. In addition, we are like two different worlds—you and your wife (may you both grow old together)—are American and I am from the old country and it is too late for me to change completely. It's true that I have entered the stage of late autumn and you are just starting your summer. It seems to me," she said thoughtfully, "that I have slept through my most beautiful years and just woke up in late fall going into winter. Autumn can be beautiful too and even winter can be wonderful, if only you know how to live . . ."

At this her tone of voice changed and she declared emphatically, "No, my son, I will not live with my children. It is not that I love you, God forbid, any less than I always have, but it is better and healthier for all when a mother is a guest . . ."

She made her farewells and left with her head held high, promising that she would come again, but only as a guest.

A Love Story

❧

SARAH HAMER-JACKLYN

Translated by Luba Cates

*M*ALKALEH CAREFULLY COMBED HER GRAY HAIR AND smoothed her wrinkled face. It seemed to her that in the three months since she had gone into the old folks' home, she had shed twenty years. Who would believe that in her late seventies she often felt like a girl? The ringing in her ears, the dizziness, had all stopped. And all because of her landsman, Chatzkel Weinstein. Malkaleh blushed: she was ashamed that a woman her age should yearn for a man.

She remembered the long-forgotten scene: a young girl living at home with Orthodox parents, betrothed to Chatzkeleh, the bookbinder's son. Then a rumor spread: Chatzkel had been seen on a Shabbes afternoon walking in the Brejner forest with Zlota, the servant girl. Malkaleh's parents immediately broke the engagement. Her tears and pleas did nothing. Chatzkel had a hobby of sketching people and animals as well; a habit they said was suitable only for a gentile or a ne'er-do-well.

A few months later Chatzkel left for America. Malkaleh married someone else—a quiet Yeshiva student—but she never forgot Chatzkel.

Years later she came to America with her husband and three children. Her husband, Zalman, became a presser in a ladies' clothing factory, but he lacked aptitude for this trade, and so they opened a candy store on Rivington Street. The children helped, Malkaleh helped, and they managed to make a living.

In America, Chatzkel's name was Harry Weinstein. Malkaleh heard that he had become very wealthy as a real-estate broker. She met him twice: once at a dance and a second time at a banquet for their landsmen. Both times he came up to her and introduced his wife, a tall beauty bedecked with bracelets and jewelry. He asked Malkaleh how she was doing. When Malkaleh's husband died, he came to the funeral. All this happened when she was still young. She never saw him again.

Malkaleh never remarried, turning down good matches. She thought of nothing except raising her children, guiding them into becoming good adults. The years flew by, the children grew up and married. Malkaleh became a grandmother. She ran her business and her home, cooked and baked. On Shabbes and holidays her family gathered about her, and she was pleased to be a mother and a grandmother.

How the years flew by! From a young girl to a mother and grandmother. Now she was a great-grandmother. With age came a ringing in her ears and dizziness. One day her daughter caught her in a fainting spell and it was resolved that Malkaleh must not be left alone. The children met to decide what must be done. They all wanted her to live with them, but in the end it seemed she had nowhere to stay. Her eldest son, a salesman of women's lingerie who was constantly on the road, was married to a gentile woman whom Malkaleh found distant and cold. The youngest son and his family lived in Boston. This son really wanted her with him, but Malkaleh felt she was too old to make a move to a strange city. The children knew that she really wanted to be with her daughter but there was no room. Her daughter and son-in-law barely made a living and lived with their five children in a tiny house with four small rooms. In the end, the only place for Malkaleh was an old folks' home.

At the beginning Malkaleh wouldn't hear of it, but after much discussion, she decided to go in for a few weeks on a trial basis. She didn't give up her house so that, if her new residence didn't please her, she could always go back. Malkaleh remembered with what a heavy heart she had come. "It's the doorway to the next world," she'd said. At the time she planned to stay only a week, but when she met Harry Weinstein—or Chatzkeleh the bookbinder, as she liked to call him—everything changed for the better. They both became as animated as if they had just discovered a newfound treasure. Harry wouldn't leave her alone, and she plied him with questions.

"Why is a rich man in an old folks' home?" His answer was that a rich man can also be a lonely man; when his beloved wife passed away, his children made themselves scarce.

"And so it will probably go with *their* children and grand-children," Malkaleh replied. "That is how the world turns. Children only need us until they're grown."

"Oy, Malkaleh, I didn't know you were so wise." They spoke at length; Chatzkeleh told her he would like to sketch her.

Malkaleh had wrapped herself in a white shawl. She glanced in the mirror and became embarrassed. A woman her age with such feelings for a man! She comforted herself with the certainty that she was not the only one who liked the company of a man, know-ing full well that the other women envied her for the attention Chatzkeleh was giving her.

Malkaleh walked calmly to the tree where Chatzkeleh stood waiting, pencil in hand. He saw her, smiled, inspected her, and said happily, "That's good." He indicated a wooden bench and said, "Sit here."

"Perhaps I should have worn a hat."

"No, no, Malkaleh, the way you're dressed, you're the very spirit of our mothers and grandmothers."

His pencil started dancing on the canvas as he told her that all his life he had wanted to draw, but who had time for such foolishness? Now it was this "foolishness" that kept him alive.

One evening they were strolling under a clear sky with the moon following them. Harry, who was in deep thought, suddenly stopped: "Malkaleh, let's get married."

Malkaleh became so upset she was speechless. When she regained her composure, she quietly said, "Have you lost your mind? You're even older than I am. Do you want people to laugh at us? What do we need to get married for? We're always together."

"It would be different. We'd have our own home. I like going to Atlantic City and Lakeview. It wouldn't be proper to take a woman who is not my wife."

"My children and grandchildren would be ashamed. They'd think I'd lost my mind."

Much as he tried to talk her into it, Malkaleh held her ground. She refused, even though in her heart she knew she was enjoying this. She thought about it day and night, and the more she thought, the more it pleased her. But whenever Harry started to talk about marriage, she had one answer: *Stop talking such foolishness.*

One day a new resident appeared in the home. News soon spread: she was Molly Wexler, the once-famous soubrette of the Yiddish Theater. It seemed many of the residents remembered her from their youth and many had sung her songs.

Molly kept them waiting till she made her entrance into the activity hall as befitted a star. For the first time there appeared in the home a bleached blond, her wrinkled face complete with eyeshadow, rouge, and dangly earrings that shook as she moved. She was gowned in blue silk, with patent-leather high-heel pumps; her blond hair had been styled in an exaggerated bouffant.

She was surrounded by all the men who remembered her from happier times. They complimented her, assuring her that she didn't look a day older, that she was still young, still beautiful. They talked about the productions they had seen her in. Molly beamed with happiness, receiving the compliments as she had once received bouquets of flowers. Among her admirers was Harry, who remembered her from his youth, as well as later on when she sang in the cabarets.

In the five weeks since Molly became a resident, she provoked a strong sense of competition among the men. They took to wearing their Shabbes suits and bright ties during the week. When Molly sang in her husky voice about old struggles, her voice was drowned by the male chorus that sang along. The women listened to the songs from a far corner of the room, looking enviously at this intruder. Feeling threatened, they had begun a quiet boycott of Molly, refusing to associate with her.

Suddenly one woman left the women's corner. She shuffled up to the choir and joined them in the songs, which she still remembered from her youth, when she had been in the choir of the Yiddish Theater. The women looked at her with disdain, as though she were a scab. They turned with pity to Malkaleh, who stood silently, her head bowed. They knew feelings ran deep between Malkaleh and Harry—and now Harry was part of the group surrounding Molly.

One day, when Malkaleh was out on her morning walk, she looked around, wondering if she would meet Harry. When she didn't see him, she wandered to the park where he liked to sketch. She was shocked to find him sketching Molly, who was dressed like some Spanish señorita in a white dress with a red shawl over one shoulder and a red rose in her hair. For a few minutes Malkaleh stood behind them and watched. She became dizzy and dejectedly started to leave. Harry heard steps and turned; when he saw her leaving he called out, "Malkaleh, Malkaleh, come here!" But she didn't answer nor did she stop. She went into her bungalow, threw herself on her bed, and quietly wept. She thought of going to stay with her children, painfully regretting that they had ever talked her into giving up her own home. Finally she fell into an exhausted sleep.

It was late afternoon when Malkaleh awoke. She stared at the portrait Harry had done of her. Outside the window a young tree was in bloom. The house was filled with sunlight which illuminated the portrait. A fly buzzed in monotone. Malkaleh's grief was profound, filled with regret that she had driven Harry away. *It's not nice . . .* and *What will people say? . . . At our age . . .* —with these words she had delivered him to Molly.

At dinner that evening Harry stopped by her table and asked why she had run off. Malkaleh blushed like a young girl. She stammered words he could not understand. He waited for her and they began to walk. Malkaleh was silent. Harry chatted away, then suddenly stopped. "Malkaleh, are you angry with me? Why?"

"Do you think I can't see how taken you are with that common actress?"

He started to laugh. "What are you thinking? . . . I like her as a model. I enjoy singing with her, and that's it. You're the only one I love!"

She felt as though a great weight had been lifted from her. She kept on walking in happy silence, then abruptly said, "My roommate keeps me up all night. The woman snores, she wakes up in the middle of the night, and turns on the lights. Does she care if she wakes me up? I'm going into the office tomorrow and asking them to change my room or my roommate."

"You won't get a new room here. And what makes you think you'll get a better roommate? Me, I'm a quiet sleeper; I'll never wake you up turning on lights. You'll be the boss of your own home."

Everything was silent; the sun went down. For the very first time since they'd met, Malkaleh leaned her head against Harry's shoulder.

"When do we get married, Malkaleh?"

"The Shabbes after the fast of Tisha b'Av . . . God willing, we should live and be well."

Bryna Bercovitch

Bryna Bercovitch (née Avrutick) was born on August 13, 1894, in the Ukrainian town of Cherson, in a slum area called the Zabalkas. She was the youngest of seven surviving children. Her father, Itzik, was a *melamed* and a follower of the Lubavitcher Rabbi; her mother, Chaya-Sarah, kept a traditional Jewish household. In the early 1920s, both parents died, and soon after Bercovitch's four brothers immigrated to North America.

Bercovitch was the rebel in the family. At age twelve, following the failed revolution of 1905, she was outraged at the conditions of the political prisoners in Karmozhne Prison near Cherson. She began reading secular writers such as Gorky and developed her political and literary views under high-school *(gymnasium)* teachers—first in Cherson, then in Kiev—who were secret revolutionaries. During these years, in Kiev, she saw Meyerhold's theater company performing Ibsen and Chekhov. In 1915, she was admitted to Shanyovsky University—a progressive open university in Moscow. In 1917, inspired by Trotsky, she joined the Red Army and fought on the Polish front and in the Ukraine, where she was wounded in battle against the White Army under General Deniken.

Bercovitch returned to Cherson and took up school teaching for a time, but soon after left for Moscow, where she studied theater and acted under the direction of Meyerhold, Vakhtangov, and Stanislavsky. She also began living with the artist Alexander Bercovitch, and became pregnant in 1922. That year Alexander Bercovitch left Moscow to teach art in Ashkebad, in Russian Turkestan, and she followed a year later with her newborn daughter Sylvia.

Another daughter, Ninel, was born in 1925. Bercovitch set up a school and orphanage and worked for the Party, but under pressure of the drastic conditions then prevailing—famine, counter-revolution, social and economic upheavals, during which Alexander Bercovitch lost his job—the family (aided by her brothers in Canada) immigrated to Montreal.

The move to the New World was a deeply troubled one: poverty, language barriers, cultural estrangement, constant moving from one slum lodging to another, and a stormy marriage. Bercovitch taught at her brother Nachman's Yiddish school and continued her work for the Communist Party. In 1933, a third child was born, a son named Sacvan (for the anarchist martyrs Sacco and Vanzetti). Three years later, in the aftermath of the Trotsky Trials, Bercovitch left the party. She retained the idealistic core of her radical beliefs, but her commitments gradually shifted to her love for Yiddish literature and culture.

Her marriage ended in 1942. Alexander Bercovitch never remarried; and although his work was widely known in Canada, he died in poverty in 1951. By that time Bercovitch was crippled with rheumatoid arthritis and other ailments resulting from decades of physical hardship and mental distress. Confined to bed after 1945, she began to write a weekly column for Montreal's Yiddish newspaper, *Der kanader adler* [The Canadian Eagle]. (*Der kanader adler* published first as a daily, and then as a weekly from 1907 to 1988.) Bercovitch's subjects ranged from reminiscences of early childhood, memories of Kiev, Odessa, and Moscow, experiences in the Revolution and as a Depression-era immigrant to short fiction, literary criticism, and commentary on current events—some one hundred pieces in all. She was hospitalized during her last years and died in Montreal's Hospital of Hope on April 27, 1956.

Bryna Bercovitch's memoir "Becoming Revolutionary" was translated jointly by Bercovitch's son, Professor Sacvan Bercovitch, and her daughter, Sylvia Ary, at the suggestion of their sister, Ninel Sigel. "Becoming Revolutionary" is a compilation from nine of the articles she wrote for *Der kanader adler* during the period from

1945 to 1950. From the perspective of the bleak Cold War era in Montreal, Bercovitch looks back at the idealism and naivety of a younger self and considers the origins of her radicalism. In the beauty of its language and the vividness of its perceptions, Bercovitch's text provides a map of the interiority of radical commitment. Bercovitch's hunger for social justice stems from the poverty her family suffered under the Tsarist regime and then is galvanized by the example of a childhood hero of her shtetl who participated in the failed revolution of 1905. The memoir follows her to university in Moscow and then to her time as a member of the Red Army during the Russian Revolution of 1917 and the Civil War that followed.

Becoming Revolutionary

❦

BRYNA BERCOVITCH

Translated by Sacvan Bercovitch and Sylvia Ary
Edited by Rhea Tregebov

A snowstorm in Montreal, Canada. The wind is wailing like a Jewish fiddle. The melody sounds familiar, close. Moods of long-ago yesterdays whirl around me; and moods, too, of the present, which is more veiled and further away than the past. Dark forebodings of tomorrow—they flash like lightning and vanish just as quickly.

It's dark outside. Through the frozen windowpane, my whole life stands before me like a specter. Is it a dream?

*

No, it really happened. I remember, first, a small, impoverished house on Kuznyetchna Street, in the town of Cherson. My days, from Sunday to Friday, dragged by slowly. Soon after I'd had my sweetened glass of tea and roll in the morning, I was tortured to tears by hunger until our evening meal. When I complained to my mother, she acted according to her mood. If she felt good, she would send me to the store with a kopek to buy a piece of herring or a slice of halvah. If she was in a bad mood, I received a slap for my whining. The meat at supper was never enough to nourish me. Even when my father gave me some of his portion I was still unsatisfied. "Look at her," my mother would say. "She's glaring like a wolf, as if she expects to be given the whole half-pound of meat."

With the little money that my father gave her, it was difficult for my mother to prepare the Shabbes, but she did it with great skill. On Thursday, she'd start for the market at the break of day, and would return tired but content a couple of hours later with a full basket. My father would greet her with a smile: "Did you bring home a whole storage-room of provisions?" "I went everywhere," my mother would answer, "and I bargained with every peasant. A hundred times I turned to leave, a hundred times I turned back, haggling over a kopek, or a half-kopek, but I have everything that we need for Shabbes. I even have something special, a bottle of the finest wine, which I bought for eleven kopeks, to make kiddush. What do you think of that?" My father would stroke my mother's shoulder and start to sing, "A good woman is more precious than jewels." Blushing, my mother would move aside, feigning annoyance: "Come now, enough of that. Leave it for Friday night."

On our shelves, perch swam and splashed in the big clay bowls. One bowl held a long, narrow pike. My mother would scale the fish, slit their bellies, and dice their intestines while the perch and pike still quivered. From another dish, reserved for soaking meat, she would take a calf's head, a lung and heart, a liver, a couple of marrow bones, and the better cuts of meat to prepare. With my wolfish eyes I imagined the meat cooked and baked. In my imagination I swallowed it greedily.

All day my mother whitewashed walls, polished windows, and scrubbed every corner. She would have preferred to clean the floors (which she'd then cover with sackcloth) on Thursday, but she left that for Fridays. My father was a *melamed,* a schoolteacher, and he used as his cheder the room next to the kitchen. So my mother would begin her washing only after my father had let out the schoolboys early Friday afternoon. Then she worked hastily. "What can I do?" she complained. "This is how we make a living."

In a deep tub, covered with an old, clean tablecloth, the kneaded dough rose. My mother baked bread for a whole week. She made *mandlen* for the Shabbes soup, flat rolls, small biscuits, and sometimes sweet cookies with poppy seeds. Friday at dawn the kitchen looked like a bakery. My mother was an expert chef. The shelf and bench were covered with baking pans and basins, her noodle board, the sieve, and rolling pin. With a couple of goose feathers my mother dipped beaten egg from a saucer to baste the twisted tops of the loaves and round rolls. She was busy with the poker and shovel, stirring the coals and glowing ashes to keep the stove red hot.

These were happy moments which I cannot forget. My stomach craved the Shabbes delicacies—the grated bitter radish mixed with goose fat, the jelly of veal's broth, the cholent with the noodle pudding.

But not every day was Friday. I remember once being afraid to tell my mother how hungry I was. I didn't want to hear her say angrily: "What should I give you? What? My misery?" But I burst out without meaning to, "Mama, I want to eat!" To my surprise, my mother took out two kopeks and said, "Here, go to Yankel the Shoykhet; buy a piece of herring, but a fat piece, and, for the other kopek, a piece of halvah. I'm faint from hunger, too, so we'll both eat." I ran, full of joy, and came back empty-handed. Yankel said he had nothing today; he told me to come back tomorrow. I was full of bitterness. "Mama," I asked, "why do they call him *shoykhet* when he's a storekeeper, and not even a storekeeper?"

"I'll tell you the truth," my mother answered. "No one really knows what he is, but he has a license for ritual slaughtering, so he's a *shoykhet*. And his name is Yankel. So he's Yankel the Shoykhet."

Yankel was the son of our actual *shoykhet,* Reb Hillel. From early on, Yankel had a reputation for brilliance. At the age of nineteen, he had been acknowledged as one who knew mystical philosophy, acknowledged not only by the chief rabbi of Cherson, but also by rabbis of other cities, those who certified him to be a *shoykhet*. Yankel took to the studies of the Torah like a fish to water. He knew the Gemara and the Tanach, as well as all the ins and outs of the ritual slaughtering knife. There could be not the slightest doubt that Yankel was fit to take on the best post when it came to the ritual slaughter of chickens and cows. But in spite of these high attributes Yankel never became a *shoykhet*. He refused every offer. Why? For what reason?

Reb Hillel said that his son could not bear the sight of blood—he'd faint if he saw the blood of a chicken or cow. Many rich men wanted Yankel for a son-in-law and offered to give him money and a place to live so that he could study to become a rabbi. But this too was rejected, not directly by Yankel, but through his father. Reb Hillel would stroke his fine, well-combed beard and answer with a little smile, "My Yankeleh doesn't want to get married yet. He says 'No way.' Go do him something. But it's alright; he'll get older, with God's help, and he'll get wiser." Soon after this, Yankel left Cherson.

Reb Hillel told his friends that he had sent his son to study at the Slobodske Yeshiva, but that was known to be a lie. People said they had seen the young *shoykhet* in nearby towns: in Lvov, Kachovka, Berislov, Nicolayev, Odessa, even Kiev. Everywhere he wore the handsome long garment and hat which went so well with his trim little beard and pious face. People related that in whatever town he came to, he would stay over at the Rabbi's house and spend several days with local scholars, show off his learning, and take walks for long hours of the day and night. Then suddenly, he'd be off.

After a couple of years, Yankel returned to Cherson, to be called up for the army. But he was set free from army duties. Doubly set free. First of all, Yankel was a first and only son, and secondly, he was a *shoykhet* and the son of a *shoykhet*. Well, fine and good. Now what would our Yankeleh do? Would he finally become a *shoykhet*? Or would he choose to be a rabbi and accept a match-maker's proposal?

Neither. "No way." Yankeleh threw off his long, black garments, cut off his sidelocks, grew a goatee, and became a store-keeper. The store he took over was a dark hovel on Kuznyetchna Street. The shutters were closed summer and winter, and so was the low, crooked door. One had to knock for a long time before Yankel stuck his head out through a crack in the door. And whatever you asked for he didn't have. Yes, he would get it later today or tomorrow, but it wasn't there *now*. He'd give you a warm, lighthearted look and then lock the door shut. In the evenings a commotion could be heard behind the locked doors and covered windows. Solitary figures would steal in from the courtyard through the back door; in and out. A couple of times people noticed someone climbing up to the attic late at night.

The men shook their heads. "Evil ones are hovering around Yankel's store. It must be that the demons and ghosts are busy there!" The women whispered among themselves: "May I be as sure to have a good year as I'm sure that Yankel is a socialist. Just like his sister. She studied and studied, and now she's in prison!"

Thus three or four years went by. During this time, Yankel went away several times for short periods. His father would look after the store and chase the children away from the courtyard. He guarded his son's store day and night.

Then, in the spring of 1905, everything changed. Yankel opened wide the crooked doors, threw open the shutters, and washed the windows. The cut-up herrings vanished from the windowsill and so did the halvah from the rusted shelves. Now a brass scale and balance shone in the sunlight. The thin, pale storekeeper stood in the doorway, and with his sweet smile and bright eyes attract-ed customers, especially women. The store was now full of fresh foods, glass jars with nuts, boxes and biscuits lining the shelves, as well as notebooks, writing paper, envelopes, ink bottles, and pens. Things became lively from morning to night. Yankel's friends, men and women, began to come in openly to talk things over with him, and then left with full shopping baskets, packed valises, small and big boxes. But the door which led to the back rooms was blocked with barrels of gasoline and heavy boxes. Yankel would slip in and out. It seemed that something was going on.

Something *was* going on. A stormy year, 1905 was full of energy and anxiety as the Socialist youth prepared for the Revolution. Their aim was clear. The working class would break the chains of slavery. The proletariat of all countries would unite in the battle against the bourgeoisie. A general strike would paralyze all industries. Across Russia they were ready for mass demonstrations, ready to fight on barricades.

Young though I was—a ten-year-old girl—I was already being drawn into the turmoil. Yankel the Shoykhet, a secret socialist, had talked to me many times. He gave me illegal books which I read in secret. He gave me important messages which I delivered proudly and with dispatch.

Long after midnight, just before the first of May, a group of policemen and Cossacks invaded Yankel's store, closed off the street, and surrounded the courtyard on all sides. The policemen pried open a door and searched everywhere. About twenty young men and women were dragged out from different hiding places. They found packs of illegal literature, proclamations, two red flags, several hectographs, loaded revolvers, and boxes of dynamite. One young woman grabbed a flag and shouted something about the First of May and the international working class. Yankel began to sing "The Marseillaise," and the rest of the Revolutionary group joined in. Bruised and bloodied, they were taken to prison.

In a few months, Yankel and his comrades were sent off to Siberia. Their heads shaved, bound in chains, they were marched to the Nicolayev train station under heavy guard. Yankel strode in the middle of the dusty street with a courageous step, his dreamy eyes fixed on the distance. Crowds of people followed along the sidewalks, among them Yankel's father, his face pale, his back bent, looking older than his age. At the train station, Cossacks on horses turned the crowds away with their whips. Many ran away, but many others pushed through, among them Hillel the Shoykhet. Whoever caught the look at that instant between father and son, their silent farewell, would never forget it.

It was in 1905, too, that the political prisoners of Karmozhne Prison rebelled. They were then tortured even more cruelly than before. I could not bear it. On a cold night I struggled through the deep snow behind the prison. No road, no light. The wind was sharp. My heart beat fast. There they were, my comrades, beaten and bullied. I seemed to hear their despairing cries. Was it the wind which made me hear the whispered "listen" of prison guards? I suffered with you, my dear friends. Though I didn't know you, my soul was with you in the night.

By 1907 I'd started reading the Russian classics, drinking from the well of Maxim Gorky's works. Thin volumes bound in red and black covers lay hidden in every room. When no one was home, or late at night, I read them with a beating heart. A thirteen-year-old girl is like an exposed nerve, open to the shocks of the world.

Seven years later, in December 1914, I was on the train to Moscow, heading towards the big city to study in Shanyovsky University. Classes had long since started. I was late, very late—the grippe had kept me home in bed. No matter, it was not yet too late. There would be enough time to catch up. I was full of ambition and courage. This was no small thing—Shanyovsky University, the most radical learning institute in Russia!—the only one of all the Russian universities that provided student aid and encouraged creative potential! They had no quotas for Jews. They had a faculty of social sciences. There was a famous professor of literature.

With my application I'd submitted two compositions—a brief autobiography and a critical study of Dostoyevsky's *Poor People*. My compositions must have made an impression because I was accepted and exempted from school fees. I was supposed to begin on the first of September, and there I was on the train in late December with my straw basket and eight rubles sewn into my shirt in a little bag. When my mother had left me at the train station, her thin shoulders shook with crying. But my heart sang with joy: I was going to Moscow! And now the wheels were clacking; the wind shook the telegraph poles and tore at the wires. Sing louder, you winds! Beat faster, train wheels: *to study, to learn, to study, to learn.*

How could I *not* go? It was my dream to study all the social sciences, literature, and philosophy. And I'd heard so much about Shanyovsky University, this wonderful, unique institution. No power on earth could stop me. I had no residency permit. But how could I worry *now* about police persecution? Hunger and Moscow frost—I knew about all of it. Also about the persecution of Jewish students. Hundreds of them lived without roofs over their heads, dragging themselves through the nights along the Moscow streets. But I wanted to be there. Why couldn't my feet serve me both day and night? For so great a cause, couldn't they make the effort?

My mother provided me with a pair of felt boots and bolstered them with fur and wadding and a big dose of motherly warmth. All through that long, terribly cold winter, I'd walk around for eight to ten hours every night and my feet never froze. My comrades would be amazed: "What sort of magic is there in your boots?" I knew what it was: my mother's warmth and my own firm resolve not to give in, not to break down. It was also the stormy spirit of youth, the need to learn, to absorb the great ideas of our time and all times.

So my feet carried me in those times, day and night, in storm and in sunshine, until the Revolution came. Then my feet set forth in a different direction.

I remained in Moscow through the fearful year 1916. The failed Russian campaign in World War I had brought death, hunger, and despair. Revolutionary parties speeded up their activities. Spontaneous, open confrontations showed that the silent masses had begun to speak out. From the newly formed Duma, there came the bold voices of Kerensky and Tseretely. The air seemed electrified. And in 1917 came the Revolution.

I see it now as a complex, multicolored mural. In the center were the inflammatory Bolshevik proclamations: "Land for the Peasants. Factories for the Workers." "Peace to the Hovels, War to the Palaces." The ironclad decrees which followed from Moscow reached into every corner of the vast and stormy country. They showed that the Soviet powers were in dead earnest: they had undertaken to make these proclamations a reality. The hope shone of a "Global October" which would set the world free.

The other parts of that Revolutionary mural were wrapped in shadows. Dark clouds were racing to cover the sun; the Russian earth was steeped in the blood of a terrible civil war; there were vicious pogroms in the Ukraine, an apocalyptic image of a doomed Revolution. More than one Menshevik or anarchist predicted the later developments of Bolshevism. But who would listen to these pessimists? I and thousands of others like me were told that the pogroms were a knife in the back of the Revolution, created by the counter-revolutionaries. We fought them on all fronts. Some of us went into the Red Army; others, the "Red Eagles," risked their lives gathering the harvest of the peasants and getting horses and cows for the soldiers. Many went to fight against the gangs of opposition around Kiev.

January, 1920: a red hurricane was sweeping over our Russian soil. I was in a Red Army unit in the Ukraine, a political Commissar. We were battling against Petlura and Denikin and their bandit gangs. The night felt hot. On the snow, I lay wounded in the middle of the field. The pain in my shoulder seemed unbearable. I believed that I would die now, but I knew that the Revolution would win. The blood from my wound took the appearance on the snow of a black bird with widespread wings. I was thirsty and, with my good hand, I took chunks of snow in my mouth. Oh, how good the cold snow felt on my palate! In my delirium, I thought I was at home. A barefoot girl on a summer day, I stand near a little wagon with a big metal can on it. A peasant in a red shirt gives me a tiny bowl of ice cream and a tiny white spoon. He smells of whiskey. He laughs and says to me, "You, little Jewess, give me a little kopek and I'll give you sweet ice cream." And suddenly, he lifts me up on his wagon. I woke up with a scream and heard one medic say to the other, "Yes, she really is frozen."

Several months later, in a rainy spring dawn, I knocked quietly on my mother's door. I was returning home on leave from the Soviet Polish front. When my mother opened the door, she saw a strange figure in a soldier's shirt with a shaved head, the left arm slung in a black kerchief. She recoiled in horror from the typhus-emaciated body: "No, it's not Bryna, it's not my child."

Later we both sat by the boiling samovar. We were drinking tea, having a bite to eat, and talking. With my mother's help I had washed and changed into clean clothing. My mother was already calmer. Sadly, she shook her head. "Is this your Revolution, my daughter?"

"My Revolution is also your Revolution, Mamma," I answered. "It's the Revolution of all hard-working people. In a year—and another year—our Revolution, like a mighty fire, will engulf the whole world. You say 'wounds, suffering, bloodshed,' but Mamma, you know how hard it is to give birth to a child. How much harder it is for a whole new world to be born! Yes, Mamma, we will create a new, good, beautiful world. No more war, no more hunger, no more prisons. Mankind will be free and happy—and in the near future! But you don't believe! You're smiling!"

"No, my child, I don't believe. And I'm smiling through the pain. Do you know why? I see with whom you're going to be dealing. Only with good people can you create a good world. And the good are like a drop in the ocean of the bad. So what can you accomplish? Even if there were another thousand like you—oh I wish that what I'm saying weren't true: I don't even want it to pass my lips!"

A month later I was already on another front in a Red Army unit fighting with a group around Kiev. When I returned in winter to Kiev and went to my old quarters in the students' residence, the Commandant handed me a letter. My brother had written me: "Sit shiva, my sister, because our dear mother died on Chanukah, on the third day. She was very lonely for you and until the last minute she worried about you. Dear Sister! May God protect and have pity on us, because here where we are there is a terrible hunger. People are dying like flies."

*

Today, on the first of May, 1950, it rained. So it did last year, and two years ago. It seems to me that for a long time now, a bright spring day has turned into a day of sorrow. Rain, tears—it's the mood of bitterness, suspicion, and disillusion which overwhelms thousands and millions. The First of May was once the embodiment of unity for the working class. The Red Flag was the symbol of the great fight with the enemy, capitalism, as well as the dawning of the future for which workers were ready to shed their blood.

Twenty years ago, on the First of May, 1930, millions of proletarians throughout the world marched in closed ranks. Their hearts beat in unison in London and in Moscow. All roads led to that Red Bridge. There, "the final and decisive conflict" would be fought. Who can forget the hunger marches in the 1930s, the May parades, the mass meetings? The spirit of rebellion united workers and intellectuals alike. Then came catastrophic disillusion, for some sooner, for others later. Believers saw the great betrayal and were left broken, shattered, neither here nor there, neither dead nor alive.

Now, thirty-three years after the Revolution, when we look into the future, we see politicians from East and West mixing poisons and preparing dynamite. The past still shines through from a distance with all the charms of truth and fantasy. For those who, with their own hearts' blood, colored the flag of the First of May, and who now see the flag crushed beneath the feet of a tyrant, for them there is still one consolation, one refuge—the wine of the past, the memory of the bright glow of youth.

Anne Viderman

−𝐆

ANNE (HANNAH) VIDERMAN WAS BORN IN THE SMALL TOWN of Oushitza in the Podlier District of Ukraine on June 20, 1899. As a child she was an avid reader, despite the poverty in which she was raised. There was a meager library in Oushitza in which many of the books were damaged or partial. Viderman would read all she could and then herself compose the missing sections of the stories, scribbling them down on scraps of paper. Viderman's father introduced her to the writing of Sholem Aleichem, who became her favorite author. She was deeply affected by the anti-Semitic scandals of the Dreyfus Affair of 1894, in which Alfred Dreyfus, a Jewish officer on the French general staff, was accused of spying for Germany, as well as the 1912 "blood libel" trial in Russia of Mendel Beilus, a Jewish tailor who was falsely accused of having murdered a gentile child in order to prepare the Passover matzos. She was a serious child who rarely played with other children and lived in the books she consumed. During the Russian Revolution, Viderman fled Russia with her family. She moved with her husband first to Bessarabia and Romania, and then immigrated to Montreal in 1924. She began writing in 1929, at the age of thirty. In June of 1939 she became a columnist for Montreal's Yiddish newspaper, *Der kanader adler* [The Canadian Eagle]. *(Der kanader adler* published first as a daily, and then as a weekly from 1907 to 1988.) Much of Viderman's writing appeared in *Der kanader adler,* including her debut article, the memoir, *"Der aynzamer kinstler"* [The Lonesome Artist]. Viderman published *Umetiker shmaykhel* [Sad Smiles] in 1946, a privately published collection of short stories, articles, and memoirs, and *Alte heym un kinder yorn* [Old Home and Childhood] in 1960, a collection of reminiscences, stories, monologues, and sketches.

"A Fiddle," the memoir included in this anthology, was originally two articles, her debut article, *"Der aynzamer kinstler"* [The Lonesome Artist], as well as a later article, *"Gvald, der redakter geyt"* [Help, the Editor Is Coming]. Both were published in *Umetiker shmeykhel* [Sad Smiles]. Music is the link that bridges Viderman's experiences from the Old World to the New. In the first section, Viderman relates her memories of the tragic death of a beloved cousin whose "hunger"—his passion for the violin—unsatiated though it was within the narrow confines of the shtetl, inspired her own aspirations. In the second section of the memoir, this passion for music with its longing and loss is transposed to Depression-era Montreal, where Viderman's own stifled musicianship obtains a brief, if ecstatic, expression again through the violin.

A Fiddle

❧

ANNE VIDERMAN

Translated by Esther Leven

THERE WAS GREAT ACTIVITY AND COMMOTION GOING ON AT my Aunt Chaya-Liba's house. They were expecting an important guest: her youngest son Motya was returning home from service in the army. My Aunt Chaya-Liba was a little old woman who did matchmaking for a living. Her husband Velvel sometimes earned a little from arbitration. Understandably, these sources combined barely met their daily needs.

Their children were scattered all over the world: in America, Brazil, and Argentina. They had been in these places so long that they had tired of writing home to their parents; no one even knew their addresses. My aunt and uncle's one remaining son, their youngest, Motya, had been taken into the army. For three long years they had waited for the blessed day of his home-coming.

Motya was olive-skinned, tall, and slim; he had a head of curly black hair and two rows of gleaming snow-white teeth. He met everyone with a happy little smile. The house was filled with cheerful noise all day long as people kept coming in—relatives, neighbors, friends, and acquaintances. Finally the greetings were over; someone reminded Motya that he'd once made himself a fiddle and learned to play it. He had been a young boy at the time; now they were asking him to play for them. Motya didn't have to be coaxed: he took the fiddle, passed the bow over the strings, and—a flood of notes poured out which captivated every one of them. Beneath his touch the strings turned into real beings: they spoke, yearned, cried, lamented, protested. Suddenly they expressed joy, wonder, and happiness—all that the human spirit can sense and experience was brought forth by his fingers on the fiddle. People sat enthralled, their eyes brimming with tears, as they listened and took it all in. Since the house was filled to overflowing, people even stood outside, listening at every window.

I was at that time a young girl of twelve. I too remained seated, enchanted. Loving music as I did, I was so charmed that I felt as if I were flying high above a flower-carpeted magical land of white-winged, angelic inhabitants. The flood of musical notes lovingly touched and caressed and promised so much, so much happiness . . . Suddenly I tumbled down to reality: all was still. Motya had finished playing. The fiddle lay across his knees and he was smiling a sad, tired smile. We heard the last faint notes linger then fade away in the air. I envied Motya so; how fortunate he was to be able to bring such uplifting spiritual pleasure to his fellows!

The weeks went by and the commotion at my Aunt Chaya-Liba's died down. Motya was no longer a guest. He seemed now to be downhearted, somehow unable to settle down. The town was too small for him; he found himself desperately hemmed in. Once when he came to our house, my mother offered him tea and cake. He pushed the tea aside, crying, "Give me something else to still my hunger! Everyone gives me tea, cake, or preserves, but no one knows my hunger . . ."

I was dumbstruck: was it possible that such a person as he could be hungry but have nothing to eat? My childish mind could not comprehend this. My mother put something on the table. As I observed how Motya ate, the ache in my heart brought me close to tears. When Motya finished eating, he asked if I would like to learn to play the fiddle. "If some day I am far, far away, maybe playing my fiddle will remind you of me," he said.

"Where are you going?" I asked him.

He stared into space. "If I should die, I would want you to have something to remember me by."

I sat there unhappily. He began to laugh, showing his gleaming snow-white teeth. Later he wrote some musical notes down for me and hurriedly began to teach me to play.

I remember one evening when Motya was giving one of his concerts: as always, the house was overflowing with people. Moise Berman, the son of the town's wealthiest man, was passing by. He stopped, listening in amazement, then ran up the stairs and into the house. When they saw him come in, everyone rose. Aunt Chaya-Liba brought him a chair and so did Uncle Velvel. The rest made room for him. It was too bad he couldn't occupy every seat at once to please this subservient, obsequious crowd.

You could see on Motya's face how the whole scenario disgusted him. A little later, a shoemaker lad who clearly also loved music came in. No one rose to offer him a seat; he stood humbly at the back. Motya stopped playing.

"Come closer; why are you standing so far away? No one's going to bite you!" he said, finding the boy a chair.

Some time later, the family started urging Motya to get married. He didn't respond, but sat there silent. But they pestered him so that he lost patience. "What do you want of me?" he cried, confused. "What right have I to marry if I can't earn a living?—why should I bring misfortune on an innocent Jewish girl? I wish I had the money to wrench myself away from here." His eyes shone with tears. I looked at him and envisioned a mighty eagle caged, flapping its wings in vain. If he were able to get out into the world, surely he would become a great artist. But what could I, a twelve-year-old child, do for him if he, who was twice my age, could not help himself?

One Friday my Aunt Chaya-Liba came over to tell us that something was wrong with Motya; he wasn't feeling well. My mother went to see him. When she came back, I heard her tell my father that she was worried about Motya. The following day the doctor was called in; he wrote up a prescription and left.

Saturday and Sunday went by and then came Monday. However long I live, I will never forget that Monday. Motya lay sick in bed. His face looked awful, dark as coal; on his head was an ice pack. He beckoned me to come closer. Though he tried to speak, it was impossible to hear or understand what he was saying. Perhaps he felt he was going "far, far away," as he had told me a few weeks earlier, when he gave me my first fiddle lesson. I leaned closer, straining with all my strength to make out even a single word from his parched lips, but it was useless . . .

I could not watch his helplessness any longer and left. As I was leaving, I glanced at his tired hands with their slim shapely fingers as they lay on the blanket. Was it possible that these fingers would be silenced forever? Dear God, I reprimanded myself, how dare I even think so?

About an hour later, when I was standing outside, a woman walked by and looked up at the porch.

"What's going on?" asked the woman.

"It's already gone . . ." someone answered from above.

The terrible lament of the old mother and father could be heard as it was joined by the weeping of everyone in the house. People came and went preparing for the funeral. They brought boards and soon hurried away with a heavy sinister burden. Done. Everything was quiet. Everyone had left for the funeral. I walked home past the large marketplace, which stood deserted and empty. I walked with slow quiet steps, my head bent, my mind in a fog. I felt as if I were in a dream. *Motya is dead!*—those three words kept repeating in my head. Observant people say, *God's will be done; God is just.* Those phrases also went through my mind, but surely in this case He had been too just—and what is too much is more than enough.

I went into my house and saw Motya's fiddle on the wall, hanging there peacefully, as though nothing had happened. It felt as though a knife had pierced my heart and I burst into a frantic, mournful wail.

*

Many years later in the city of Montreal . . .

It was a summer evening.

I was sitting in Fletcher's Field. It was quiet, the air was cool, few people were about and I sat sad and deep in thought.

Suddenly a group of French-speaking boys and girls appeared.

A couple of them were wearing overalls and torn shoes. The girls were unkempt in dresses of an indeterminate color; all were about twelve to fifteen years old. One boy was carrying an accordion, another a mandolin, and yet another a fiddle.

They all sat down on a couple of benches and began to play. Not one showed any particular talent. I sat there staring at the fiddle and I got a sudden urge to take it. I was filled with an overwhelming desire to play.

I came up to them. "I can play the fiddle a little."

They all turned their heads and observed me with hurt in their eyes, clearly thinking that I was making fun of them. They didn't believe me.

But the boy with the fiddle came up to me and asked, "Do you want the fiddle?" And he handed it to me.

I looked around to check that no one was watching and took the fiddle from him. Everyone gathered around me as I started to play a type of Russian folk song.

They all started to cheer up, smiling at each other as if to say, *See, Madame does know how to play and we thought she was joking.* A few passersby joined them, then more and more enlarged the circle around me. I played a waltz and people made requests: *Can you play "O Canada?" "God Save the King?" "Ramona?"* Requests came in from all sides and the crowd seemed very exhilarated.

Suddenly it seemed to me that I saw my editor not far from us. *Help, what can I do, where can I run from these raggedy boys and girls, where can I hide?* These thoughts raced through my mind, but God took pity on me, for I was mistaken. It was another young man who, from a distance, in the dark, seemed to resemble my editor. A weight was lifted and I breathed easier. But I was afraid to go on playing, for what if someone were to see me and report to my editor that they had seen me at Fletcher's Field with a group of raggedy boys and girls playing on a fiddle for them? Who knew what kind of impression this would make on my worthy editor? For such behavior he might stop publishing my work in his newspaper . . .

The truth of the matter is that I feared no one as I feared my editor: first God, then my editor.

I hurriedly handed over the fiddle and said goodbye to my young friends and was on my way. I could hear disappointed and confused comments from the bunch.

"Why, Madame? It's so early!"

A couple of the girls were actually clinging to my hands.

"Sorry, I must go," I replied, freeing myself from their hands and from the circle of people gathered around us. I hastily got further away in the dark among the trees.

Such a sweet evening: I laughed to myself like a naughty child. I won't ever forget that evening.

Malka Lee

DESPITE THE TRADITIONAL CHASSIDIC BACKGROUND THAT LED her father to burn her early poetry, Malka Lee (née Leopold) persevered in her desire to be a writer and went on to publish more than nine books of poetry and prose. Born in the town of Monastrich in Eastern Galicia on July 4, 1904, Lee escaped Poland with her family during the First World War and settled in Vienna. In addition to her mother tongue of Yiddish, she became fluent in Hebrew, Polish, and German, and graduated from the high school *(gymnasium)* in Vienna. Her family returned to rural Poland in 1919, after the War had ended.

In 1921, Lee immigrated alone to the United States at the age of sixteen. Although as a student in Vienna she had written poetry in German, in New York she soon returned to writing in Yiddish. She documented her experiences of leaving her family and adjusting to life in North America in her memoir *Durkh kindershe oygn* [Through the Eyes of Childhood], published in 1955. The book was dedicated to Lee's family, who perished during the Holocaust. Lee married writer Aaron Rappaport, with whom she had two children, Joseph and Yvette. Lee soon gained a reputation as a writer in the thriving Yiddish literary community in New York. She completed her studies in New York at the Jewish Teachers' Seminary, Hunter College, and City College. In later years, Lee went back to visit Europe; she also traveled to Mexico and Israel. During her stay in Israel in 1960, she became involved with Pioneer Women/ Na'amat, and began to assist in the organization's projects in the United States. Her books were published in New York, Buenos

Aires, and Tel Aviv. After Rappaport's death, Lee married Moshe Besser in 1966. *Mayselekh far Yoselen* [Short Stories for Joseph], a children's book published in 1969, became one of her best loved and best known works. Lee's poems have been set to music for chorus and piano by the renowned Canadian composer John Weinzweig. Malka Lee died in New York on March 22, 1976.

Though it is difficult to imagine a child audience for this story, "The Apple of Her Eye" *[Shvartzepel]* was included in *Mayselekh far Yoselen* [Short Stories for Joseph]. Set in the New York of the 1920s to which she immigrated, Lee's portrayal of a widowed working-class woman's anguished and heroic efforts to raise her children in the slums bears witness to a New World no less brutal to the impoverished than the Old.

The Apple of Her Eye

✌

MALKA LEE

Translated by Esther Leven

$\mathcal{T}$HE APPLE OF HER EYE FIRST CAME INTO THE WORLD IN A dark basement below the El. The racket of trains drowned out his first cry. He was born as blue as ink. His mother lay there, her eyelids the shade of night.

The pounding of the everyday sounds of pedestrians, trains, and cars echoed above them, resounding through the earth to their cellar below. A small basement window facing onto another window separated night from day; all the windows were covered with dirt, all strained for sunlight so the day might shine through.

A few days after Sonny was born, his mother put him into his eldest sister's care. She was six years old and she was to watch over him and give him his bottles. His father had died at his job digging subway tunnels: Sonny's mother dreamed he would grow up to be different—stronger, more free. She would not give *him* up to the earth.

Every day she went to work and left the children to look after themselves. They watched the baby as he kicked his legs or drew them up from cramps. They would stuff his mouth with bottles to keep him from crying, but he would turn away and cry even louder, and then they would all start crying helplessly along with their little brother. At night his mother would come back worn out from a hard day's work, but Sonny, no longer attached only to her, would turn to anyone who went to comfort him.

Winter came. The cellar became damp and humid from the leaky ceiling. The children were all sick in bed. When Sonny cried, a neighbor's child came in and picked him up like a doll; Sonny shut his eyes and fell asleep.

*

Days turned into weeks and weeks became months. His mother worked every day and every day came home weary, burnt out as an ember. Sonny would smile his toothless smile at her. She would kiss him, kiss his hands and feet, and warm his whole body till morning, when daylight would again take her away to some stranger's house to earn her family's daily bread. But one day a week—Sunday—was happy. On Sunday, Sonny's mother would not go out to strangers' homes but would spend the day cleaning her own home and preparing for her children's needs for the week.

Sonny would watch the little window, which brought him regards from the daylight behind it which was not allowed in . . . The child stared wide-eyed at the bit of light making its way into the small dark home. It was a hard winter. Wearing silver boots with sparkling spurs, the frost came and covered the windowpanes with frosty branches; the sky was like a sheet of gray metal showering silver sparks of snow. Sonny's eyes grew whiter, as if the daylight had gotten in and then shone through them like small white windowpanes. The children played with him. He could smile now and point to the little beam of light forcing its way through the window into their house. His small legs were weak; he couldn't stand up on them. His bones were soft as dough. The dampness had entered his bones and he wasn't able to get up to walk on his leaden feet . . . his mother was in strangers' homes, washing the floors and shining the windows, washing clothes for other children while hers were dirty, naked, and hungry.

*

In those wealthy people's homes hung pictures of landscapes, forests and hills; landscapes which breathed with the warmth of their artists' hands, with the secret of immortality.

Sonny's mother, dusting their frames and staring at them, dreamed of taking her children to a green field where they could fill themselves with sky and sun.

Days and years went by. Sonny had his third birthday. As spring drew some of the moisture from the walls, their basement home began to dry out. But the city paved more asphalt, the earth was shut down and could grow nothing, and though it strained, no one paid any heed. Sonny was drawn to the blue strip of light which shone a little brighter through his small window. His head seemed as big as a pumpkin, but his legs were even thinner and he wasn't able to get up to walk. Only his hand gestured towards the beam of light.

One day his mother was walking home, tired as always, her hands red from all the washing. She walked slowly. She felt a pain in her chest and stopped to rest by some shops. The shop windows were full of the best of everything. You could buy anything for only ten cents: a little sock for ten cents, a glove for ten cents, all kinds of delights. She took it all in. She stopped in front of a picture—a blue sea and a blue sky with a ship in the middle rocking on waves so sunny it was as if the sea were on fire. She kept looking, imagining herself on the ship with the boy and the rest of her children, all of them sailing together to a land full of light. She took ten cents from her purse. She would buy the picture and bring it home and hang it on the wall across from Sonny. She would bring the sky to her basement.

As she paid for the picture, she asked the salesclerk whether a mistake had been made, because she'd seen these kinds of pictures on wealthy walls and had been told that they cost much more. The clerk wrapped it up for her in a parcel and gave it to her for her ten cents. Finally she was home. She had to stoop as she went down the twisted wooden stairs to the basement. She opened the door.

Sonny was alone. It was dark. No lamp had been lit. The other children were at the neighbor's. He had been filled with dread—he'd been left all alone in the dark—his mother would never come back—fear came at him from every corner. He was about to burst into tears, but suddenly—what was that? In the darkness a blue light began to show, the kind of blue light which hid on the other side of the window. A red sun came into view.

Sonny reached one leg over the side of the bed, then the other; then the first leg touched the floor and, enchanted and happy, he began walking unsteadily toward the blue light, his arms out-stretched and his legs trembling, till he touched the figure of his mother with the blue picture in her hand. She held him in her arms and the sky came down to that dark room.

Frume Halpern

❦

FRUME HALPERN WAS BORN IN 1888 AND IMMIGRATED TO THE United States in 1905. She was known as a proletarian writer not only because, like the protagonist in "Blessed Hands," she worked as a masseuse, but also because her writing is informed by her commitment to left-wing political causes. The stories are also infused with a profound and nuanced psychological insight into the moral and ethical dilemmas her working-class protagonists experience. Although Halpern's stories were published for over forty years in the left-wing daily newspaper *Morgn frayhayt* [Morning Freedom] and, in later years, in the literary quarterly *Zamlungen* [Collections], as well as in numerous anthologies, her first collection of short stories, *Gebentshte hent* [Blessed Hands], did not appear until 1963. Halpern was by then in her mid-seventies. *Gebentshte hent* was published by a committee of prominent writers determined that Halpern's work not "languish in newspapers," as they noted in the preface to the book. Halpern died in New York in 1966 at the age of seventy-eight.

All three stories included in this anthology, "Three Meetings" *[Drei mol bagegnt]*, "Blessed Hands" *[Gebentshte hent]*, and "Goodbye, Honey" (the Yiddish title is transliterated English), were originally published in *Gebentshte hent* [Blessed Hands]. "Three Meetings" unfolds during the era of "Bread and Roses," the tumultuous period at the beginning of the twentieth century when workers in the New World, immigrant and native alike, struggled not only for their livelihood but for the most basic civil rights. The setting of Halpern's story is the events leading up to the 1911

Triangle Shirtwaist fire, a notorious and tragic event in labor history. Having immigrated to New York a few years earlier, Halpern would have been twenty-three at the time of the fire. Her readers in the left-wing daily newspaper *Morgn frayhayt* may well have lost friends or family in the tragedy. The fire broke out at the nine-floor factory in the Lower East Side of New York City. One hundred and forty-six workers, most of them Jewish and Italian young women, died either as they leaped to escape the flames or in them. The factory was in the middle of a labor dispute and the owners had locked the doors to keep union organizers out. Although Halpern's text refers to the "almost three hundred" killed in the fire, this figure represents the total number of workers in the factory, not the actual number of victims.

"Blessed Hands" is set much later, in post-war New York City, where the masseuse's patients include frail Holocaust survivors as well the Park Avenue wealthy. The protagonist, like Halpern herself, has made the transition from shtetl to New World, but her new life poses a challenge to the Old World values she has carried with her.

"Goodbye, Honey" continues Halpern's sensitive and complex investigation of class barriers, as well as sexual politics, as they are expressed in mid-century America. Molly's marriage to a wealthy, much-older husband rescues her from a life of drudgery, but it proves a Faustian bargain. In this story, the Old World casts no shadow, but the brave new world portrayed is one dominated by the "fine golden net" of mercantile values.

Three Meetings

❧

FRUME HALPERN

Translated by Roz Usiskin

THE FIRST MEETING TOOK PLACE THE DAY FRAIDEL CAME to the women's garment factory in New York. Everything was new to her and strange. The people, the work: nothing was as she had imagined it to be. Though she knew how to use a treadle sewing machine, she'd never before used or even seen an electric machine.

Earlier, friends had warned Fraidel not to let on that she didn't know how to operate an electric machine. The woman who brought her into the sweatshop seemed to suspect as much. She led Fraidel to a machine, gathered a bundle of silk cloth, and sat her down to sew, asking Fraidel whether she knew what she was doing. When Fraidel nodded, the woman smiled and went away.

What's to know? It's simple, Fraidel thought. But when she set her foot on the pedal, the machine sprang into motion like some wild mustang. Ashamed and frightened, she quickly took her foot off the pedal. Surely the women beside her had seen and were laughing at her? But no one stared at her; they didn't even turn their heads. She couldn't see their faces, since they were all busy tending their work. She fought the machine, but no matter what she did, the machine refused to obey. The pieces of cloth were no better; they all looked the same to her.

She sat dazed, unsure what to do next. Surely someone would notice her and come to help? But it was no use. She couldn't catch anyone's attention.

Not far from Fraidel's machine, a bit to the side, were three machines set in a T-shaped formation. Three Jewish girls were working at these machines. One of them was an attractive blond curly-haired woman. Fraidel's searching glance caught her. The blond girl was bent over her machine, her body swaying rhythmically from side to side. While her left hand rested on the machine, she quickly fed the cloth with the fingers of her right hand. For the blond girl, work was effortless. She could keep up a rapid conversation with the other two girls at the same time. The threesome were clearly enjoying their discussion as they worked, and this made Fraidel even more unhappy.

She sat there forlorn, not knowing what to do. How envious she felt of the other, happier girls, especially the one with the beautiful blond hair. It was clear that for the blond girl, work was a lark; she chattered away constantly.

The girls beside Fraidel had to be deliberately refusing to look at her! They saw her as some pathetic greenhorn.

Her powerlessness was all their fault! The feeling gnawed at her. Slowly her jealousy and anger turned to self-pity. If she hadn't been ashamed, she would have burst out crying. How could they be so mean? Didn't they care about anyone else, about someone who sat so close beside them suffering?

She grew angrier by the minute. She made up her mind: under no circumstances was she going to work in this factory! She buried her face in the bundle of cloth; slowly pressing down with her foot, she tried to control the wild machine so that it wouldn't jump the way it had before. This was how, with great difficulty, she survived to lunch break, when she stood up to leave the factory. As she moved to the door, Fraidel could hear the blond girl say, "We're making progress! See how we're progressing?!"

"Progress" was a forward-looking thought, an intelligent word, Fraidel decided. Those girls were intelligent. *Who knows,* the thought suddenly struck her, *maybe it's my own fault that the girls didn't notice me? It was just a mistake, I should have appealed to them for help!—but no matter what, I still won't work here!*

*

Years went by. Fraidel had long forgotten about the girls. She had her own problems and no time to think about the world beyond herself.

One Saturday afternoon, Fraidel heard someone yelling, "Extra! Extra!" She ran down to the street and bought a Yiddish newspaper. There was a lengthy report on the fire that had destroyed almost three hundred young lives, mostly girls. Fraidel became as distraught, as disturbed, as if it were her own life that had been in danger. She envisioned the girls encircled by flames; saw them as they leaped from windows. She couldn't tear herself away from the newspaper's depiction of the details of the gruesome tragedy. These wretched scenes burrowed into her soul and would not let her rest.

In the morning, Fraidel stood at her window, unable to tear her gaze away from the workers passing by, each girl going to work carrying her lunch. She cried for each, as though each were going to her own funeral.

Fraidel became inconsolable in her grief. She found solace only in her two small children.

A little later, she read that a demonstration was being organized in memory of the victims of the Triangle Shirtwaist Company fire. She left to join the demonstration.

It was a cold gray day. A light, fitful rain started and stopped. Fraidel had come too early; the demonstration hadn't begun. She wandered the streets. A few others were roaming casually about;

how could they seem so blasé, so indifferent and cold to the tragedy? Some were laughing and boisterous, as though nothing had happened. Fraidel hurried from one street corner to the other, until she heard the sounds of an approaching band. She was already tired from wandering about and bone-weary from the wet and the cold. With her last bit of strength, she pushed her way through the crowd, wanting to be closer, wanting to grasp the entire tragedy.

The vanguard of the demonstrators who were marching represented the mourners for the victims—those children, daughters, and brides. Here were the parents, fathers, mothers, grandfathers, and grandmothers who had lost their children and grandchildren. Fraidel was dumbfounded by the black procession. Heads bowed, the people in black shuffled wearily in step with the funeral music. Fraidel felt as though every hair on her head were standing on end. Tears threatened to choke and stifle her.

Slowly, the procession began to change; younger people came marching with brisk steps, their heads held high, resolve on their faces.

A flame of red flags warmed the cold day. The flags fluttered upward, reaching towards the clouds. To Fraidel, the workers' flag seemed to represent their unity and their strength: it was an unbreakable shield that would defend everything, everyone.

Three young boys carried a flag. In front of the flag bearers, a young man and two girls marched. One of the two looked familiar to Fraidel; she recognized her immediately. It was the attractive blond curly-haired girl from the old sweatshop! She recognized her by the same rhythmic sway of her body she had had before, when she sat sewing at her machine. The blond girl's face showed a deep earnestness. Her step was determined. Fraidel imagined that very soon she would hear the blond woman mouth the words, *We're making progress!*

Fraidel felt small and inconsequential compared to the blond woman, just as she had in the sweatshop. Again, she started to feel sorry for herself. There she was, standing alone, merely observing this tragic scene, while the other marched with such resolve.

*

Several more years elapsed. A Saturday afternoon; Fraidel was coming home from work. It was an afternoon in May. She felt free and easy in body and spirit. It was May, spring, and the weather was warm. Tomorrow was Sunday and she wouldn't have to work. She'd soon be on her own street and she looked forward to being met by her children.

She walked at a steady pace observing the trees which only yesterday, it seemed, had been barren and raw. And now, a wealth of greenery! There in the park, it seemed that Shavuot was evident in every leaf of every tree. Wouldn't it be wonderful if Shavuot could last the full month, Fraidel thought.

At the exit to the park she noticed a woman sitting huddled on a box. She couldn't see the woman's face, but the blond curly hair reminded her of someone. Yes, it was her again, the same woman from the old sweatshop! The blond woman was sitting with her bony knees pressed tightly together. Her elbows rested on her knees, while her hand shielded her eyes from the sun. When she saw Fraidel, she turned round on the box, wanting to say something, but, realizing that this was a stranger, she fell silent.

Fraidel no longer looked at the abundant greenery in the park. For a long time, she stood looking at the blond woman, wanting to make sure that this was really her. She could no longer see what she had seen earlier in the blond woman's face. The blond woman sat uneasily, her gaze fixed on the horizon, as though she were reliving her experiences, past and more recent.

At any moment Fraidel expected the blond woman to toss her curly hair and utter those same words she had heard at the machine, words embedded in Fraidel's memory: *We're making progress!*

Fraidel felt that the woman sitting huddled on the box, knees drawn up, had moved to a place far beyond Fraidel herself, a woman lost.

Blessed Hands

୭ନ

FRUME HALPERN

Translated by Esther Leven

*E*VER SINCE SARAH HAD FIRST STOOD ON HER OWN TWO FEET and become an independent individual, her hands had been constantly in touch with human bodies; her fingers skillfully alleviated human pain, seeming to merge with those aches caused by heavy physical strain. Her hands were thanked and blessed by many mouths in many different tongues. Sometimes they were blessed by tears, sometimes by a smile.

Sarah didn't particularly care how her hands looked. She didn't think there was anything special about them except when she was working with them. With their big muscles and prominent veins, their wrinkles, their broad palms, her hands were not very feminine—truly not pretty hands! But when they came in contact with the human body, her hands seemed to take on a life of their own: they were kind and uncanny in their devotion and determination to ease aches and alleviate pain, in their desire to help both children and the elderly. Those hands reached out not only to the ailing parts of the body, but, it seemed, to the very soul.

Through these two unattractive but capable hands, Sarah often came in contact with people who did not speak her language and could not converse with her. Her hands became her medium; through them the sick could feel her intimacy with the very depths of their suffering, sickly limbs. In their eyes Sarah could read word-less blessings. These unspoken blessings became a stimulus and a force in her, as well as the root of her compassion, which she bore for many years for all who suffered.

Year in, year out—people were the same. Her fingers did not judge nor did they discriminate. Suffering is the same for everyone. When people are in pain, they moan. A broken limb is broken the same way for everyone. But still each person has a certain unique-ness, something which makes them different from everyone else.

Sarah often thought that not only did she feel for the sick, but that, through her hands, the sick could understand her feelings. They sensed her sympathy, saw how she absorbed their anxieties. The sick therefore brought her not only their own wounded lives, but also their children's and grandchildren's troubles. In this man-ner, she became entwined with everyone's families. She looked upon them as kin.

An old woman who looked like the mere shadow of a being—her skin like parched earth, the touch of a friendly hand on her body long forgotten—felt the intimacy of Sarah's compassionate touch and opened up to her. How many of her children had per-ished in the gas chambers the old woman did not know, but she did know how many of her grandchildren had. She talked about them, and the tears fell from her eyes onto the hands where they mixed with Sarah's tears, and the old woman became close to her. She blessed Sarah and thanked her, and thus Sarah became part of her family.

The old woman reminded Sarah of her own mother, her moth-er of the blessed hands. Her mother had been sick for a long time, suffering severe pain which kept her from sleeping. The children were helpless. Sarah, who was about ten, was frantic to help her mother. Her childish fingers began caressing her mother's neck; this worked like magic. Her mother dozed off. From that time on, she was always able to put her mother to sleep by stroking her with her fingers. Every time her mother opened her eyes and saw her youngest smoothing her hair, she would say, "A blessing on your hands, my child."

But it was God's will that those hands should earn a living by touching people's bodies. It was also meant to be that Sarah should share the blessing of her hands. For those who were most needy, she was able to spare only minutes; the rest of her time had to be given to those who could afford to pay. But the few minutes she gave to those whose need was greatest were given with much devotion. The old, sick, and broken were charged a minimal amount. However, for those who could pay for her time, there was no set fee. They chose a time convenient for them—too early for card playing or shopping.

Those from the working class, with their heavy, awkward gaits, were not always clean or well-mannered, nor did they often seem especially bright, but if you dug below the surface and removed the outer shell, you would find a shining humanity that took you by surprise, making you feel small and unimportant in comparison. There were, on the other hand, the polished privileged refined ones whom God had kept from all harm. There, if you removed the shine of the refined covering, you would find a little worm, a parasite.

When Sarah tended them, she had to be dressed up clean and fresh, had to look fancy for the doorman who let her in. When she walked through the lady's house, she had to tiptoe, to speak quietly, delicately, deferentially, as though she had come to beg for her livelihood. The elegant lady would be all smiles and pay her banal compliments and Sarah had to smile back in return for these compliments.

This particular lady had a lot to talk about. She complained about being tired from thinking so much, especially about her problems with the servants! *They aren't paid enough! They don't know already how much to ask for! And it's a problem, since there's no get-ting away from them.* It was hard on her nerves. The lady stretched out like a lazy spoiled cat and couldn't stop yawning; *it's too much already; let it stop; let them leave her alone!*

While Sarah worked on the lady lying on her low soft bed between silk and satin sheets, while her hands manipulated the soft body with its pudgy limbs and she listened to her prattle, she remembered her own days. She wanted to demand her own private life right here next to this person who had bought her hands and forced her to listen to her foolish chatter. Sarah thought and asked herself what, for instance, she would be doing if she were in her own home. Firstly, she would see that her children went to bed on time. She would lie down beside them and help them fall asleep, telling them a story the way she should have, except that she always kept putting it off because she didn't have the time.

Sarah was reminded of her own unfortunate mother in that poor long-ago shtetl. Her mother had to sell her own baby's breast-milk, serving as a wet nurse for the rich. She had to let her own child languish while the rich child fed at her breast. She had to give away her love for her own baby to a stranger's child. Sarah roused herself from her thoughts. She felt as though she had woken from a dream and was afraid: had she perhaps been thinking out loud? Had her thoughts been heard? Her fingers conveyed her thoughts, acting like musical instruments through which her feelings for others were transmitted. She recognized this in people's eyes. Her hands were vibrating tones, silent music! She chided herself for the time she had let slip. Rigorously, with all the tenderness in her soul, she started to pour this into the power of her hands, which would guide her on the right path. The hands in their compliance knew only one way—the truth, even for those who did not see another's truth.

The stillness in the room was blue and silken. The air was filled with a blue lassitude. The quiet musical tick-tock of the crystal-framed wall clock—which had hung in this elegant home on Park Avenue for several generations—the ticking of the clock synchronized with her breathing and with the rhythm of her fingers as they glided from one spot to another. Sarah's legs trembled a little as she bent forward. The little dog that dozed in a satin padded bed stretched out and yawned. This was no ordinary dog. It looked like a clever mistress who knows all the ins and outs of her domain. Sarah liked dogs, but this creature looking at her with human eyes was not to her liking. It seemed to her that the dog watched her and followed her movements with suspicious eyes. Each time she saw him yawning and sticking his long pink tongue out, showing his little white teeth, his silky hair, Sarah imagined that this dog felt important and wanted to flirt . . . When her work was finished, Sarah found it hard to straighten up, but she didn't want the dog to observe this, so she gathered her strength and straightened out with a gesture as if she were throwing off a weight.

The lady turned over to face her. She stretched her smooth body and a little smile of pleasure appeared on her face. With her eyes shut, she pictured herself and said, as though she were talking to herself: *what blessed hands; what magical hands!*

Sarah quickly put on her coat and hurried outside past the doorman. She had the feeling that she had just done something foolish, that someone had tricked her, and she was a little annoyed with herself. She hurried along uttering a curse out loud and ran home.

Goodbye, Honey

❦

FRUME HALPERN

Translated by Esther Leven

THE SUN MADE ITS WAY UNINVITED THROUGH THE HEAVY double silk drapes, making its appearance first on the floor, then on the tip of the cornice at the top of the large mirror and then quickly leaping to the bed. Tiny streaks of sunlight stole their way into the sleeper's eyes. The long fiery threads of light tickled her eyelids mischievously. She moved her head as if to shake off a fly. The tickling persisted, and she opened her eyes, but immediately shielded them with both hands. The sun grew bolder and spread its bright rays into every corner of the large room, greeting her with a lovely sunlit morning.

It was still early, just ten o'clock, too early for her to start her day, but she was no longer sleepy. She felt fully awake, as if she had been up for some time. Strange . . .

She threw off the covers and stretched pleasantly and thought. The self she saw in the mirror that hung directly across from her bed looked a little puzzled, as if she were asking: *Is this really me? Yes, me.* Her bright face suddenly darkened, as if she had remembered that she was about to take a rather unpleasant-tasting medicine. She cleared her throat and called, "Honey! Honey!"

From the next room she heard, "Yes, Baby; coming!"

She heard no footsteps since the floors were covered with heavy carpeting, but the more delicate pieces of furniture trembled. An old man of seventy appeared, dressed for work. He stood there, not bold enough to approach, waiting for her to call him again. She said nothing, but reached out to him. He walked slowly, his head slightly bowed. His yellow, beefy, clean-shaven face looked a little hurt and guilty. He took one longer stride, bent forward, and kissed her on the lips she raised to him. The kiss—an unsuccessful one—left them both in an unsettled position. She covered her face with her hands; he looked down, as if he were suddenly embarrassed.

As she covered her eyes with her hands, a feeling of pity for him which soon turned to one of anger came over her. Where did this old man get the nerve to buy her? Did he pity her? He was the lucky one!

He placed a very warm hand on the back of her neck. She took her hands from her eyes, saw his look of slight embarrassment and entreaty; she saw also that he was trying to tell her something and that his look was one of pure devotion. She regretted what she had thought about him. She smiled, and his face lit up.

"Today we're going to eat at the best place in America! You hear, Baby? Top-notch."

"You're good to me, Pops," she answered.

He smiled sheepishly and shook his finger. "Not 'Pops'! It makes me feel old when you call me that."

"Then it's 'Honey'! Honey, tell the girl to make me something to drink, okay?"

"Right away. I'm off."

He turned around quickly, pretending to hurry and looking rather ridiculous, and again the thought came: *such a pity.* A pity for whom?

It was only six weeks ago that she, Molly the hairdresser, had become Mrs. Carson. For many years she'd been Molly, plain old Molly. No one called her by her last name. Molly was also the name of her business: Molly's Beauty Salon. It was not an elite salon, just a small shop. Molly herself was the whole business.

She had been widowed young, with two small boys. From the few dollars that were left from a small insurance policy, she had learned the trade and become a "business" in a remote suburb. Molly had worked hard, very hard.

Molly was still young and beautiful and her beauty was a great asset to her business. The women believed that Molly could make them as beautiful as she herself was. They kept complimenting her, and the more compliments she received, the more she tried to please with her beauty. For a woman, beauty can be a great asset, but for Molly it meant not enough sleep and more hard work, more than her strength could bear.

She modeled for her business, trying out all the new hairstyles on herself. Her hair was naturally curly and of a lovely brown color, and the women were enchanted. But despite all her charm, she had to work long hours, and she stayed poor. She was never able to treat herself to a vacation. She wouldn't go alone, because who would look after her children? Taking them along cost too much money. She waited for the day when they were grown. But when the day did come that they were grown up, too much of her own good looks and strength, and even some of her hopes, had been put into the ladies' heads and their hairstyles. When her boys finished their schooling, she still had only her own two hands to depend on.

The years flew by, and Molly felt that she had to latch on to something before it was too late.

She would come home tired. Her feet felt heavy, her bones ached, and her eyes held no spark. Just getting up became harder every morning. *Wait, don't run so fast,* she begged the clock, *it seems like I just shut my eyes and the clock hands have already moved ten minutes ahead!*

So it went, day after day, week after week, endlessly. Finally, some relief arrived. One son came, looked at his mother, and said,

"It's no good, Mother. You mustn't put your whole life into those women's coiffures. You have to look to the years still ahead of you." Molly had often thought the same: faster, faster, before life escapes and it's too late! What could be done?

Molly had heard a lot about Florida. In Florida you became younger! There, a person could acquire a new life! The important thing was that poor ladies could find "boyfriends" there—not just lovers, but many an elderly man who would like to marry a nice younger lady. True, Molly didn't look the way she used to, but she still possessed a lot of charm, especially if she was rested and dressed up in the right outfit. She suddenly saw the sun and the ocean, with her in a lovely bathing suit, the men's hungry glances following her. She had almost forgotten how to enjoy a man's company. Since her husband's death, so much of her life had been spent among women only. She often thought that those women had deadened her feelings, the longing of a woman for a man.

Molly was already past forty when a new, late spring appeared for her.

Those same women who came to her salon had more than once enthusiastically told her, "Have you heard about so-and-so? She met a sugar daddy!" In her own heart, Molly never compared herself to so-and-so. Who was she and what was she, to go looking in that way? She smiled to herself: *I won't put myself on the market to be on sale. I'm going to Florida for the sunshine and to catch my breath and be myself again, so my sons can have a lovely mother and not a worn-out workhorse.*

It wasn't easy for her to say goodbye to the business that had helped her raise two sons without anyone's assistance. But she felt that she could not continue for much longer with her work. The salon had taken too much from her body and soul.

After a short rest, Molly went shopping for clothes; she felt she was doing it for the Molly who for years had known no rest. Her habit of modeling for her business was still with her. When she finally reached sunny Florida, she felt like her old self again.

Florida seemed magical to Molly. So much sunlight and so much time. It was better and more beautiful than her wildest dreams.

Could that really be her? Was it her in the mirror with the bright eyes and pleasant smile? She compared how she looked now to how she had looked a while back and was filled with pity for herself and those like her who lived an unfulfilled life.

The first few days on the warm Miami sand by the ocean, Molly was in a fog. The women who lived in her hotel suspected that she was not quite right. She seemed remote. But when Molly turned up one day, clear-headed and full of smiles, they accepted her into their circle. It was there with these "good-time" ladies that she met him.

At first it made her angry when the women pointed him out to her—this broad, heavy-footed man with the small, pale eyes, whose protruding upper lip made him appear sullen, angry, and embarrassed—saying, "You see that fine gentleman? He's for the having." She was ready to tell the ladies what she thought of them: she considered them foolish and empty-headed, with nothing to do but gossip about everyone. Why did she have to socialize with them at all? She had run from such women. However, she caught herself thinking, *I've waited so many years for this vacation and espe-cially to try to better my miserable state of life.* And a little voice whispered to her: *Don't fool yourself. You know you came here hoping to find something.*

She said nothing, pretending she hadn't heard them. The next day, when the burning hot sun started to cool and the beach became less crowded, when some of the hotel ladies had left to play cards or get ready for their "dates," it was then that Molly felt bored. What was she to do?—she didn't know how to play cards. In the midst of her thoughts, *he* appeared behind her. She became a little rattled, as though he had heard her thoughts. She was prepared to tell him that she wasn't lonely and that she had somewhere to go, but he didn't give her the chance to speak. He asked her out for dinner, as though it were to be taken for granted. He looked at her with a kind of hidden joy and said, with a click of the tongue, "You look beautiful." His round face seemed to become rounder. He thrust his hands into his pockets, then took them out again, as if he were looking in his pockets for words.

Molly was not the only one in the restaurant who was sitting with an old man: there were even younger women with older men. The old guy knew where to take her. She noticed that he had an open and easy smile; that he was no stranger to this restaurant. He was well acquainted with Miami. Obviously, he must have a good business here.

Molly's escort revealed all his colors to her, the nice ones and the unattractive ones.

His name was Mr. Carson. He had been a widower for many years and owned a whole street of houses in the Bronx. How did he become so wealthy? It was a long story. He had had a small grocery store, had saved and put away money, lived in poverty, done all the work himself—but a grocery store cannot make you rich. But then God sent the war. From his hard-earned savings of $1,000, he started to buy houses. Bought and sold, and one winter he bought and sold the same houses three times. How did he learn this business? Money teaches you. His wife, however, never enjoyed this wealth. She didn't want people to talk and wouldn't even wear the mink coat he bought her for $1,200. Then the Angel of Death came along and—one, two—she was gone. Mr. Carson's heavy lips trembled. He looked down at his pale, puffy hands and Molly noticed a tear drop down to his white silk shirt. She was touched. He was sorry that his wife couldn't enjoy this wealth. What she had had to put up with until he became rich . . .

When he was through talking, he took her hand and looked at her with moist eyes. His look was one of sorrow and pleading pity. His face reminded her of a dog sitting near a table waiting for someone to hand him a table scrap. *How many different faces could one person have?* she thought.

The next day Mr. Carson came to sit beside her on the verandah. Dressed elegantly, he didn't look as awkward as before. He invited her to go for a walk by the ocean and asked if she would dine with him again that day. She took her time accepting, but accept she did. And even though she was a little annoyed that he seemed so certain that she would accept, she didn't say anything. Good, she would go.

Soon they were the subject of gossip. The women said, "She's no fool." The men said, "An old man, huh? And he picked such a beautiful young wife. But of course, when he owns all of Tiffany Street, who can measure up to him?"

Later he didn't have to ask her. She would be waiting for him. Every day he surprised her with something nicer and better. Wherever they went, she encountered undreamed-of luxury.

Mr. Carson had opened a small crack and then the whole door to a magic world for his lady! Cruises, concerts, dances. Everything was loud. One rich affair was overshadowed by the next. It was a contest between wealth and pleasure.

She was not bored by him; they were never alone. Molly didn't think about yesterdays and tomorrows. She forgot her age. The ocean waves swallowed up the years. She felt so light she could fly.

More days and weeks passed by than Molly had planned. Her finances were starting to dwindle, and even though the season had not ended, the hotel had more vacancies. A cold joke it seemed to Molly: what, go home again, back to the women's heads in the salon? A cloud passed over her tanned and rested face.

Mr. Carson, too, started preparing to go home. He stood before her and talked like a businessman. He could promise her much happiness, he said. He had more money than he could use. His only son was rich and not in need of his money. He promised her she would be his Queen of Sheba. She would have a nice home, a maid, jewelry. He took out a small parcel containing diamonds. "See this? I don't want to know your age and you won't ask me mine."

Molly looked at his broad swollen face. She noticed that his lower lip trembled with every word spoken; she saw him look directly into her eyes, not wanting to miss the slightest movement on her face, seeking to take it all in like one who is haggling and wants to be sure he isn't being tricked.

When she saw his face light up, taking her silence as agreement, she turned her head aside. A painful, angry feeling came over her: he was rejoicing already. She felt as if little worms were crawling over her. But soon the thought entered her mind—back to work, to heads, setting hair till late at night? How much longer could she take hearing about someone else's happiness, while she dragged herself home, trying to make the remaining bit of strength in her bones last? No! No going back!

Molly carried within her two different feelings. On the one hand, the feeling of being rescued: no more beauty salon! No more women's heads! This filled her with a kind of holiday feeling. On the other hand, she was afraid of becoming entangled in a web of lies; a fine golden net, but a net nonetheless.

They arrived in New York together as man and wife. Quietly, without any fanfare, Molly had traversed the great distance from an ordinary beauty salon on an obscure little street to Riverside Drive. It was quite the journey!

However, Molly felt that he had got the better bargain, not she. For almost two months now she had been Mrs. Carson. Carson had not exaggerated his wealth. He owned more than what he had promised her in marriage. She was not surprised by his personality, either. He was soft, spineless. He had even tried to learn how to dance the tango for her sake. Molly had to laugh when she saw the old man trying to dance this exotic dance with her.

At home, he was quiet as a puppy dog for his "Baby." But when he went over to "his" street, he became a different person, walking with a different gait and talking in a different voice.

There, when he was talking with the tenants, the painters, the plumber, the janitors—there he held his head high and his word was law. He walked out of his house quietly, but when he saw the chauffeur, he was no longer the quiet old man, but the boss.

They had been living together for almost two months now, but the time seemed to pass slowly. Even though she spent little of her time at home, the days seemed empty . . . just two months and what lay ahead? Inside her was a sadness, a longing for something. Her eyes wandered over the luxurious room. A ray of sunlight played over her bare foot like a naughty kitten. Was he gone already? Good, if he was gone. She wanted to make sure that he was no longer in the house, so she rang a little bell sitting on the table beside her bed. A young, slim girl entered with a glass of fruit juice. The girl had brown skin and smooth blue-black hair and a small pretty face. She walked on tiptoe, swaying as she walked, and was neatly made up, as though she had dressed up just for her mistress. She handed Molly the glass and looked on with a sweet smile. Molly envied the girl her ease, her fluttering movements. It seemed to her that the girl looked at her with scorn in her eyes. She would have liked to say something to the girl to put her in her place, but she said nothing. She told the girl to put the glass down on the little table and asked her if the boss had left. The girl answered yes, and Molly nodded, indicating for her to leave. As the girl walked away, Molly watched tight-lipped, feeling a throbbing in her neck.

Mistress Carson was annoyed with herself for asking the girl to bring the juice to her bed. She imagined that the girl had looked at her as if to ask: *since when have you become such a princess? Why do you get to order fruit juice in bed?* Molly became upset with herself and with the girl. She quickly realized that the girl hadn't meant anything. Molly had only imagined it. *Being a mistress suits me like a top hat on a cat,* she thought.

She soon answered her own question, thinking, *I asked for the glass of juice so I could be sure that he had gone. I can't stand the way he looks at me.* But again thoughts of the girl came back to mind. Tomorrow or the day after or the day after that she would have to meet the girl's eyes with their strange look. She would send her away immediately, today.

The phone rang. "Hello. Hello, Honey? You're coming home soon? Yes, yes. I'll be ready! Goodbye, Honey."

Yes, Molly thought, the girl must go. She couldn't do it herself, but he . . . he would do it for her. Goodbye, Honey.

Rochel Broches

❦

ROCHEL BROCHES IS THE AUTHOR OF A BROAD LITERARY OEUVRE which includes short stories, novellas, plays, and children's stories; the critical recognition she achieved saw her works translated into Russian, German, and English. Broches was born in Minsk on September 23, 1880. Her father, a follower of the Jewish Enlightenment, schooled her in Hebrew and Torah. When she was only nine, Broches began writing a journal. Her father died that year and, as the eldest child, Broches had to start work as a seamstress to help support her family. She later taught needlework at the Minsk Jewish Vocational School for Girls. When Broches was nineteen, her first short story, "Yankeleh," appeared in the monthly Yiddish periodical *Der yud* [The Jew]. The difficulties Broches experienced during her childhood are reflected in her writing, which speaks eloquently of the plight of the impoverished and oppressed. Soon after her first story was published, Broches married; her husband was a dentist. The couple relocated to a village in the province of Saratova on the banks of the Volga River. Although Broches continued writing in this isolated setting, it wasn't until the family's return to Minsk in 1920 that she reconnected with the Yiddish literary community and began again to see her work published in such journals as *Fraynd* [Friend] and *Tsukunft* [Future]. She published a number of volumes, including *A zamlung dertseylungen* [A Collection of Stories] in 1922, *Nelke: dertseylungen* [Nelke: Stories] in 1937, *Adlerl un Shloymele* [The Eaglet and Little Shlomo] in 1939, and *Shpinen* [Spinners] in 1940. Her collected works, containing over 200 short stories, along with other texts, was being prepared for publication by the State Publishing House of White Russia when the Germans invaded the Soviet Union in 1941. The book was never issued. Broches died in the Minsk ghetto in 1942. A monument carrying the words *Untern barg* [Beneath the Mountain]—the title of one of her stories—stands on the mass grave where she is buried.

Rochel Broches' "Little Abrahams" *[Avremelekh]* was published in her 1940 short story collection *Shpinen* [Spinners]. The setting in pre-revolutionary Tsarist Russia reflects Broches' own impoverished childhood. The poverty and oppression that Jews experienced under Tsarist rule was no doubt the economic determinant of the cruel "care" the children receive from Baba Bryna. Such a perspective would certainly have had the imprimatur of the Soviet regime under which the story was published. However, the story may also convey Broches' own critique of a troubling, and much debated, aspect of religious custom and law. The term *mamzer* is key here. Although *mamzer* is generally used in common parlance to describe any illegitimate child (the English equivalent would be bastard), Jewish law distinguishes between children born out of wedlock to unmarried Jewish parents and those who are *mamzers*—children born out of incestuous or adulterous liaisons whose parents are thereby prohibited from ever marrying. (It should be noted that *mamzer* is also used pejoratively to refer to any untrustworthy person, and, paradoxically, can furthermore be used as a term of endearment for someone who is clever.) Under a strict interpretation of the law, those defined as *mamzers* are allowed only to marry other *mamzers*. Under this view, the stigma is passed on to their children, and their children's children, who remain *mamzers*. According to some interpretations, *mamzers* are viewed as "spiritually wounded." Baba Bryna's caustic description of the status of the *mamzer* (". . . they aren't really children. They're dust, garbage . . .") might be a reflection of a harsh interpretation of this aspect of religious law, under which *mamzers*' "spiritual defect" is seen as generating their severance from community.

$\mathcal{L}ittle\ \mathcal{A}brahams$

ROCHEL BROCHES

Translated by Arnice Pollock

The story is new—but difficult to believe.—*Griboyedov**

ONCE, THIS WAS ONLY A CEMETERY PATH. IT WASN'T PAVED AS it is now, the streetcar didn't go by here, and the large, many-windowed factories were not here either. All around was only an empty path; very few people lived in the district.

To the side stood a lonely little house. The old rotting roof hung over the only small window, almost touching the muddy earth. The house was surrounded by potholes and ditches that made it impossible for a wagon to come near or for people to come in.

Evenings were even sadder than days. But during the day and during the night, you could hear mournful cries coming from the house; it sounded as though cats were mewing.

*Epigraph (originally in Russian) from Alexander Griboyedov's *The Mischief of Being Clever.*

Even now, you can hear moaning coming from inside. A stray dog who lives in the ditches runs up to the house, looks into the low, dark window, scratches at the window with his paws and barks sadly.

The crying from inside doesn't stop. The dog circles the house, sniffs, and barks and looks around on every side.

Suddenly, there is some movement near the ditches, a small dark shape. Yes, she's coming, she's arriving, the mistress of the house, Baba Bryna. She hears the cries from the house and swears to herself and curses, "Oy, may sickness take them, an end to them, death, the whole street is full of them!"

She doesn't hurry. She reaches the door. The door is not locked. She goes inside, it is dark. She lights a small lamp and looks around. Nothing has changed, the same familiar crowding, the low loft is practically on your head, the only bed is in its place, cries and howls come from that bed.

There, in the bed, in the huge pile of rags, are feet and hands moving, heads with contorted faces, gaping mouths. Baba Bryna looks and looks at the heap, then turns from the bed and says, "Well, Avremeleh, are you coming or not?!" And since nobody answers, she crouches under the bed and pulls something out. You can't tell by the way she acts whether she is pulling a cat or dog, but "it" is howling loudly and trying to get away from her. But Baba Bryna is determined. She quickly turns the creature bottom up and starts to spank. "Take that, take that!" she says. "You are not to eat the Avremelehs' sugar soothers, the soothers, the soothers, you Avremeleh, the soothers, the soothers, you greedy thing, you thief, you little *mamzer!*"

The noise and screaming in the house gets louder because the creature that is being spanked is yelling, Baba Bryna is yelling, the pile of creatures in the bed are screaming even louder, and the dog outside is banging on the windowpane with its paws and barking angrily.

Baba Bryna puts her hand to the kerchief on her head and tugs at it. At once, the little creature senses that he can get away. He quickly tears himself from her hands and, screaming, runs under the bed and hides.

Baba Bryna doesn't go after him. From a basket hanging on the wall she takes some bread and begins chewing it. She chews and chews and spits the bread into soiled napkins and pushes them into the open mouths of the screaming creatures. The screams cease immediately. You can only hear the quick sucking and smacking of small lips. The crying from under the bed also stops. Baba Bryna looks at the floor, where two troughs with rags are standing. In one trough, under the rags, you can see two small faces. They are quietly and weakly whimpering. Now that the screams from the bed have stopped, you can hear the whimpering from the trough. Baba Bryna is standing over the trough holding two more soothers in her hand, but she doesn't give them the soothers. She waves towards the trough and says, "It'll be the end of these two anyway today."

"Avremeleh, Avremeleh, come here, Avremeleh." The little creature doesn't crawl out.

"Avremeleh, listen to me: come out, come out." There is no answer, so the old woman crouches down as she did before and pulls the little boy out. She stands him on the bench, lifts his shirt, and examines her punishment. Yes, big red welts cover the child's body. The old woman shakes her head. "What will happen now? What am I going to do with you? You little thief!" Then she wipes the little nose so hard that the child staggers back. "Now, kiss the strap and repeat what you're supposed to say!"

The child kisses it fearfully and stammers, "No more eating the Avremelehs' soothers." Baba Bryna reaches for a wooden comb and combs and pulls at the child's curly blond hair. He sits quietly and doesn't cry out. When his hair has been combed and his nose wiped for a second time, she spits on his face and wipes it with his shirt. She finds another shirt and some socks and begins to dress him. The child suddenly remembers something, his face brightens, his beautiful blue eyes begin to shine. "We're going, we're going; hurray!"

"Such happiness, oy you little *mamzer*, you're smart enough alright!" Baba Bryna covers his head with a rag, picks him up and wraps him in her cloak. She blows out the lamp and starts to walk. As they walk, she tells him, "Remember, Avremeleh, if you bite, Baba will spank!" The child repeats quietly, "If you bite, Baba will spank!"

The old woman climbs over the ditches, swearing angrily. Then, past the dark alleys, she reaches the lighted streets. The little boy peers through the rags at the bright windows and marvels. "Baba, Baba, see the bright lights, look, look!"

And now the old woman climbs some stairs and enters a house so bright and warm that Avremeleh has to squint. Baba Bryna stands him on the floor and says to somebody, "Well, I've brought the child."

A woman is lying in bed, another woman sits beside her, and yet another woman is standing—all three inspect the child.

"He's too big, he won't do. He has teeth, he'll bite."

"Well, Avremeleh," says Baba Bryna, "what do you say?"

The child answers, "If you bite, Baba will spank!"

"Ha, ha, pretty smart," they say, laughing.

"Very clever," says a pleased Baba Bryna. "A *mamzer* has to be smart!"

It doesn't take long and they lay the boy next to the woman in the bed. They uncover her swollen breast, the dark red nipple can scarcely be seen. The child lies quietly and waits.

He puts his mouth to the breast and quietly and carefully begins to nurse. The woman sighs, she is already feeling more comfortable. She looks right at the child, thankfully and with a gentle maternal tenderness. Her hand gently strokes the curly head. "What a lovely child," she says, and starts to stroke his entire body.

The child shudders, stops nursing, and says, "Ow, stop!"

The woman lifts the child's shirt and what does she see! "Oy, my goodness," she cries. "Look, this child has been beaten—what happened?"

Baba Bryna, sitting nearby, responds coldly. "What should I do with these little *mamzers*? A *mamzer* is a thief! This little boy, as soon as my back is turned, steals the soothers from the babies and eats them!"

The little boy listens to the complaints, he is busy nursing, try-ing very hard not to bite the nipple. His eyes are shining. His lovely eyes look into the woman's eyes and the woman also looks into his eyes with concerned tenderness. It is the look of a mother who is nursing her child; it is also the look of a small helpless child who is lying safely and quietly at his mother's breast. These are beautiful moments which belong only to them.

The others are busy listening to what Baba Bryna is telling them. And what can she tell them?

Well, she takes care of these unfortunate children—discarded, abandoned, nobody wants them—little *mamzers*, no father, no mother—you understand these children never had a father. And the mothers? They aren't mothers, either. They throw these infants away wherever they can, under a fence, in a barn, at her doorstep. She feels sorry for them, gives them a place, a bed. Please under-stand she is paid for doing this, she has to live too. She takes care of the child. She will certainly go to heaven, because who would take these children in if she didn't? They would be lying around on the street, in a barn, in the alleys, because they aren't really children. They're dust, garbage, that's what everybody believes and that's what happens. Are you going to say it isn't so? Well, then, why don't you take them into your homes and take care of them?! Sometimes, the mother will send something for the child, but, of course, she has no obligation! Baba Bryna herself never had any children of her own, but she has to take care of other people's! How's that for justice! It's true, the children do get to nurse—if a woman has too much milk and she can't get relief, or if a breast is infected and she doesn't want her own child to nurse, just like this woman here, Baba Bryna brings these children and they nurse. "Take this little Avremeleh, who is lying here in the bed and nursing like a prince. What, I ask you, should be done with an Avremeleh like him? He's growing, he's healthy, he has all his teeth—he really can't be used for nursing any more—what will happen to him?"

"Oy! This Avremeleh? He's a good child, a beautiful child!" the other women exclaim.

"So what if he's a beautiful child?" Baba Bryna repeats. "By all means, one of you take him, *you* raise him. A beautiful child: just pretend that one of your children has a twin!"

"What are you saying?" the women say anxiously. "Who needs a stranger's child? It's hard enough to take care of our own children."

"So, you see," says Baba Bryna, "nobody wants him and you tell me, *take care of him.* Do I have a husband who supports me? Have I as nice a house as you? Do I have nice furniture, an oven, dishes, everything I need? Yet you say to *me—a beautiful child, take care of him!*"

"Nobody is saying anything," say the women. "We just said Avremeleh is a beautiful child, it's a pity . . ."

"What do you mean, 'pity'?" says the old woman. "If his mother and father threw him away, who is obliged to take care of him?"

Avremeleh has finished nursing. A drop of milk sits on his lip and he licks it off with his tongue. Finished. They take him away from a mother's warm arms, from a mother's warm bed. His dream has ended, his sweet, childish dream. He stands on the floor in his short shirt and socks and looks around. Everybody looks at him. He is a little boy, not quite two years old. Now he is a little full, but the woman who was like a mother to him wants them to give him something else to eat. The other two women, however, try to talk her out of it. He has to be hungry so that he will nurse better. Nevertheless, they give him a piece of a bun. He eats it quickly, chewing, crunching his teeth.

He stands by the bed where he was so happy and looks around. Everything here is so wonderful, such straight walls, such bright lamps.

"Oh, oh, oh," the child murmurs in wonder. "Ah, ah, ah," he says softly. Suddenly he cries out, "Baba, Baba, look, Avremeleh, an Avremeleh is sleeping," and he points to the infant lying in the crib.

"What's he talking about?" ask the women, and Baba Bryna explains that all her boys are called Avremeleh, little Abraham—that's the name they are given at the bris by the shammes at the synagogue. All of them are called Avremeleh.

"What are the girls called?" they ask.

"The girls don't have names. You can call them whatever you want. Sometimes the mother will give the child a name, but most of the girls don't have names. It doesn't matter, because their births aren't registered, or their deaths. Nobody looks for them, not when they're alive or when they're dead."

"Garbage," one of the women whispers. "Truly garbage."

Avremeleh doesn't understand the adults' conversation. He stares at everything around him with wonder and joy. "Oh, oh, oh," he exclaims at everything, pointing at things as he gazes. "Oh, oh, oh." He has finished eating the bun, but he bends down and finds a crumb that he dropped and pops it into his mouth. He doesn't want to move from the bed. He's tired and he's full. He crouches down and crawls under the bed. Shh . . . Avremeleh has gone to sleep . . . shh, shh, Avremeleh is sleeping.

Baba Bryna finished talking, went into the kitchen, and had a bite to eat, and went back home. Avremeleh stayed for a few days.

*

Here's how Avremeleh lived in the house for a few days. He wasn't hungry. He nursed a few times a day and ate other good, cooked food in a bowl. Not knowing how to eat with a spoon, he ate with his fingers, lapped with his tongue, and nursed with his lips. He patted his stomach happily, clapped his hands. He felt so good. They dressed him in a warm shirt and, to his great joy, shoes! The shoes weren't even a matching pair—a neighbor provided them. One shoe was tied with a lace and the other had a button. He was so delighted that he would stop after a few steps and murmur, "Shoes, shoes . . ."

Somebody gave him a little paper box as a toy. His eyes gleamed with delight but he didn't know what to do with it. The box opened and closed, he poked his fingers into it. Oh, isn't this wonderful? He collected discarded matchsticks and put them in the box. He didn't leave it for a moment. He slept with it pressed to his heart. He slept on a bench near the stove, he had a pillow which he patted and hugged.

His lovely face filled out, the color in his face brightened, his body became heavier. He would stand at the open door of the room and eagerly look around . . . he saw people, everyone was good to him, everyone knew him. "Avremeleh, Avremeleh," they would call, and give him a candy or a cookie. He would grab it and put it in his mouth. He didn't want to leave this place; he loved it. He remembered how things were . . . The adults also remembered . . . perhaps they were ashamed of how this small, helpless, abandoned child had been treated . . .

*

And then Avremeleh didn't know how long it had been. He thought that he had been in the house a long time; he was so comfortable with his life that he thought he would always stay there. But the woman, whom he has loved and in whose arms he is so happy, has gotten better. Now she needs her breastmilk for her own child. Avremeleh has looked at this baby many times and can't understand why this child is here and not with the other Avremelehs at Baba Bryna's, sucking the soothers and screaming day and night. This Avremeleh here would often be at the woman's other breast nursing, and the happy mother would baby-talk to him. Everybody loves this Avremeleh, they rock him and bathe him. (How Avremeleh gaped at this.) They kiss him and pat him. (How Avremeleh gaped at this.) He would watch them and cry out, "oh, oh, oh," and point with his finger. It was as if he were saying, "Look what's going on! One child has everything, the other, nothing!"

And then the time comes when he has to leave. Baba Bryna

comes to take him away. Avremeleh tries, in his fashion, not to be taken away. He hides under the bed and won't come out. As they try to pull him out, he cries, "No, no, I don't want to go to Baba, no, no."

So Baba Bryna, in her usual manner, calls to him, "Avremeleh, pay attention, come out or I'll get a strap! Come out!"

But Avremeleh cries and won't come out. The grown-ups pull him out. He is taken away screaming. "Goodbye, you're a good little boy, but you don't belong here."

*

And now he's back in his old home. The little boy remembers: *Yes, here's the trough where I slept, and here are the troughs where the others sleep.* But now the space is empty. Avremeleh sees that there are no children there. He points and says, "Nobody! No babies!"

Baba Bryna answers angrily, "No babies! They're in the cemetery. You'll soon be there, too."

Avremeleh is holding in his hand a bagel. They had given it to him at the house. He hadn't eaten it because he was full. Baba Bryna takes it away from him. "You greedy thing, you ate enough while you were there! Give it to me!"

The Avremelehs in the bed are screaming, Avremeleh remembers now, yes, this is home, he knows; he sees the strap on the wall, the dog's face in the window; yes, he nods his head—this is home. "Oh, oh, oh," he nods his head.

Baba Bryna is chewing bread and making soothers. Yes, soothers, remembers Avremeleh.

Now he remembers everything. He's tired and crawls into his trough. Baba Bryna puts two new Avremelehs into the other trough in place of the missing ones. In the middle of the night, he wakes up as the old woman is putting a new Avremeleh in the trough beside him and another one in the other trough.

Someone is lying in the bed, crying and sighing. "Sleep, sleep, Avremeleh, this has nothing to do with you," says Baba Bryna.

He falls asleep. When he wakes in the morning, he sees somebody in the bed. It's not the other woman, the gentle one, the one he loved; this is a different one. She is holding a new Avremeleh, and he's nursing. The old woman says to her, "Nurse him, nurse him, you'll get lots of milk and you'll nurse the others, too." She places the other Avremelehs at the new mother's breast. But he is not to nurse. "You're too big," they tell him. "You have teeth. You can eat other things." But what does he get?

Later, when all the Avremelehs have nursed and it is nice and quiet, Baba Bryna goes out and Avremeleh talks to the new lady. He shows her his shoes, he shows his paper box, he tries to tell her about his lost good life.

"Far from here," he says, "a table, cookies, candy." The new lady gives him a piece of bread, kisses him, and says, "You're a sweet child," and starts to cry.

Avremeleh likes her, he pats her with his little hand and says, "Don't cry, don't cry; Baba will spank!" And they become friends, the little boy and the lady who cries often, when Baba Bryna goes away. The nice lady nurses all the Avremelehs and they don't scream as much. She gives him a piece of her bread. She cuddles and kisses him and when he plays with his shoes or paper box, tells him how smart he is.

But then he awakes one time and she's gone. The bed is empty, she's not there, but the Avremeleh that came with her has stayed. While she was there, this Avremeleh was quiet, he slept; but now that she's gone, he is screaming. Baba Bryna is pushing a soother into his mouth, but he doesn't want it, he spits it out and screams. The old woman says, "I'm going to throw him out, let the dog eat him!"

"Don't, no," says Avremeleh. "Cold outside!"

"I'll throw you out, too," Baba Bryna says angrily. "I don't need anybody."

Later the lady comes back. The milk is hurting her. Where is her Avremeleh? But Baba Bryna has already taken him away, he's not in the house any more. The lady cries and cries. Avremeleh goes up to her and pats her and says, "Don't cry, don't cry; Baba will spank."

Baba Bryna says to her, "Foolish woman, why are you crying? You need him like a hole in the head. Did you want him to suffer?"

*

Baba Bryna is walking the streets. The Avremelehs are left alone, they scream. Avremeleh shows them his shoes, his paper box, but they are foolish, they don't understand him. They scream, make faces, wave their hands and feet. The soothers are thrown away, sucked dry. Avremeleh has taken the dried crumbs out of two soothers and eaten them. He was going to take a third one when he remembered the old woman's threat and the strap. He sighs but he wants food. He's already chewed up and swallowed a piece of paper, he's bitten off a piece of his shirt and chewed it up, but he's still hungry. He sits in his trough and cries. The dog is banging on the window with his paw and barking.

When Baba Bryna comes back, she sees immediately that the soothers have been undone and are empty. But she says nothing to Avremeleh. She doesn't touch the strap and doesn't scold him. But early the next morning, she lights the lamp and wakes Avremeleh. "Get up, *mamzer,* let's go."

The child is still sleepy but "let's go" means a treat. He rubs his eyes, gets up, and waits. The old woman gives him a piece of bread, puts a kerchief on his head, wraps him in her cloak, and leaves the house. She walks a long distance. He's drowsy. Here comes the street with the ditches. Now there are some shacks. A goat is bleating in a yard. Here comes a dog. Now there are some nice houses but no people to be seen. Another street, another street. Baba Bryna stops and puts Avremeleh down.

"Here's a porch. Sit down and sit still until I come back for you." And she takes out a bagel and gives it to him. "Sit and eat."

Oh, a bagel! Avremeleh grabs it with both hands.

"I'm cold," he says, and his face twists with the cold.

"It doesn't matter, you'll soon be warm; sit and eat." And the little boy obeys. He sits on the porch of the house and eats. He eats and waits. The old woman will soon be back.

The bagel is half-eaten when Avremeleh suddenly notices something. He becomes frightened and looks around. All the houses are shuttered and closed; he's all alone.

"Baba, Baba," he begins to cry fearfully, and starts to run around. But where will he run, where has she gone, Baba? He cries, "Baba, Baba." His shoelace comes undone and he falls down. Dust fills his open screaming mouth as he falls. Dust flies into his tear-filled eyes. He gets up, runs, and falls again. He cries pitifully. The shutters of the houses open. "What's happening? A child is crying! A child has been abandoned! Oy, a child!" People gather around. People going to work stop to look. "Oy, a child, a lovely child, whose child is it? Oy, abandoned, left alone!"

People are in a rush; they have no time. They pause for a moment and go on their way. The child stays. Some stop, look, and shake their heads . . .

The child cries and runs one way, then the other, "Here, this is where Baba went . . ."

People shake their heads. "Too bad, too bad. What a shame."

Paula Frankel-Zaltzman

꩜

PAULA (PESIA) FRANKEL-ZALTZMAN WAS BORN ON FEBRUARY 23, 1916, in Latvia in Dvinsk (now Daugavpils). She received both a religious and a secular education and worked as a bookkeeper. In 1941, Frankel-Zaltzman's home of Latvia was part of the Soviet Union, having been annexed in 1940. The 1939 non-aggression treaty signed between Hitler's Germany and Stalin's Soviet Union meant that the Soviet Union initially was not at war with Germany. On June 22, 1941, despite the treaty, the Nazis invaded the USSR. Latvia soon fell under German occupation. When the Germans invaded Dvinsk, Frankel-Zaltzman was 25 years of age and was living with her husband of three years and her parents. On June 29 deportations began and Frankel-Zaltzman's husband and two brothers, along with many others, were rounded up. Frankel-Zaltzman, her mother, and her invalid father were among Jewish civilians forced into the newly formed Dvinsk ghetto. She saw her husband and brothers only briefly afterwards; she learned later that they had been shot and killed. Frankel-Zaltzman at first managed to remain with her mother and invalid father, who was paralyzed and unable to speak, to assist them with the daily search for food and safety.

Although both parents, her husband, two brothers, and much of her extended family died during the war, Frankel-Zaltzman survived the ghettos of Dvinsk and Riga as well as the concentration camp in Shtuthof. She was working in a factory in Tehoren when she was liberated in 1945. Frankel-Zaltzman wrote *Heftling #94771: iberlebenishn in Daytshe lagern* [Prisoner #94771:

Experiences in a German Camp], the memoir from which "A Natural Death" is excerpted, just after the war while she was recovering
in the Fernwald camp for displaced persons in Munich, Germany.
Although she wrote in Yiddish, she had to type the memoir in
the Latin alphabet because no Yiddish typewriter was available in
the camp. After she'd joined her sister Shifra in Montreal in 1947,
Frankel-Zaltzman was encouraged by Moshe M. Shafir, a teacher
in the Jewish People's Schools and the Jewish Peretz Schools (and
himself a well-known Yiddish poet, author of many volumes of
Yiddish verse) to have the memoir privately published. Shafir also
painstakingly transferred the transliterated typescript back into
Yiddish (Hebrew) characters and edited the text. With the assistance of a committee of supporters from the Ladies Auxiliary of the
Latvian Mutual Aid Association of Montreal, the book was issued
as a private publication in 1949. It was warmly received not only
for the literary qualities of Frankel-Zaltzman's account, but for the
conscientious detail with which she recorded the events and people
she encountered. From 1953 to 1957 Frankel-Zaltzman lived in
Israel; she also visited Mexico.

"A Natural Death" has been excerpted from the much longer
text of Frankel-Zaltzman's memoir. The excerpts we have included
begin on July 25, 1941, when all Jewish civilians were ordered to
leave their homes and make their way to the ghetto.

A Natural Death

❧

PAULA FRANKEL-ZALTZMAN

Translated by Miriam Beckerman

On July 20, 1941, we heard that a ghetto was being established for the remaining Jews in Dvinsk. On July 25, Saturday morning, all the Jews from our shtetl were ordered to enter the ghetto. We hurried along. Father was put onto a wagon that we had managed to provide for him, and Mother and I, holding hands, made our way to where we were being sent. Resigned, we went along, without any of our clothing, without anything. The heat was torturous. We followed the wagon as one follows a hearse. From a distance we saw the gray, half-destroyed buildings, terrible to behold. From these historical buildings, which once belonged to the Romanovs, the ghetto had been made. There all the Jews of the town were squeezed in. People lay one on top of the other and it was suffocating. We just managed to find a spot to put Father down on a piece of bare earth. There wasn't even anything with which to hand him a drink of water. To add to our troubles, it began to rain. Mother steeled herself and gave me courage: "God will have mercy.

Surely he won't let such a sick old man die in the rain."

I scurried around like a poisoned mouse, looking for a somewhat better place for my parents. But wherever I looked I was tormented by the sight of the crowded, dispirited Jews who didn't even have a spot for their tired bodies. But no good would come from just walking around broken-hearted. I decided that I must not return to Mother empty-handed and tell her that I wasn't able to find us a spot—I had to find a spot—that's all there was to it. Suddenly, I saw our doctor, Dr. Rosenblum, who had tended to my father for some time. "What's to be done?" I begged him. He approached another doctor, Dr. Gurewitz, who also knew us very well, and they both whispered to me in secret that if I were prepared to work with the sick, they would provide me with a place for my father. I promised to do everything I was asked to do, as long as I had a place for my father.

We set up the second floor for those who were ill, and there, on the hard floor, my father also was given a spot. We were nonetheless happy that he would no longer have to lie on the bare earth, the wet earth. We hauled him up to the second floor practically over people's heads because there was not even an inch of free space. Mother stayed with him and I went off to people I knew to look for a bit of water for them both. Possibly it would be God's will that I would find people more fortunate than us and they might even give me a piece of bread as well. I was lucky. An acquaintance of ours, Fraida Sher, who owned a bakery, had managed to bring into the ghetto a sack of flour as well as a cooking burner and other small items. In addition, her married children worked for Germans. She gave me a glass of tea and a piece of challah for my father and told me to come again because as long as she had anything, she would give it to us as well.

My joy at being able to bring my father a glass of tea and challah was indescribable.

My job was to watch over the sick and assist the doctors. The work was hard but I didn't mind because, firstly, it meant that my parents didn't have to lie on the ground and, secondly, it was good to help those lonely unfortunates who might—who knows?—possibly today, or maybe tomorrow, be sent to their deaths. The number of the sick grew from day to day. The children caught infectious diseases and dropped like flies. My mother was no longer allowed to lie on the floor near my father, so I had to find another spot for her. Beneath our sick block were filthy stables. I cleared away the dirt with my hands and on the cold hard floor made a place for my mother. I didn't even have anything to spread out underneath her. With no changes of clothing to be had, the lice crawled freely on everyone. Whenever I could leave the hospital area for a few minutes, I would go down to Mother. With a smile and a joke I would take her aside, take off her rags and delouse her lovely white skin. As I did so, I would wonder how long it was possible to bear this. My mother became jaundiced from the stable air and suffered stomach pains from the watery soup. The raw bread that they threw our way (because that was all we deserved, since sooner or later we would be shot), she wasn't able to swallow.

At three o'clock in the afternoon, on the dark day of August 18, 1941, we were all told to line up in the yard: we were being taken to Nuremberg, Germany. Mother and I went down into the yard and lined up with all the others. Each of us was interrogated separately. When my turn came, I said that my mother was with me because I worked in the hospital. The murderer asked if I was telling the truth. Then he told me to stay but Mother had to go. Falling to my knees, I began to plead with him to allow my mother to stay, but it did no good. "If that is so, then I will go with my mother," I said.

At this point Mother began begging me to stay. "You must remain alive, my child. Who will watch over him if you don't?" She thought only of Father; it never occurred to her that she was going to her death. I didn't want to obey her, but she put her arms around me and said, "Stay here with Father, my child. I'm ready to be sacrificed for you." She was torn from me and I was thrust aside. I wanted to hand her a piece of bread that I had in my pocket, but a German shouted to me that she would have enough bread. I replied fearfully that I knew what kind of bread she would be given . . .

I watched as my mother disappeared from sight. I wanted to get one last look at her, but she didn't turn around. I only saw from a distance how she took an old Jewish woman by the arm because she didn't seem able to see where to go . . . I was again forced back into the hospital. Wretched, I ran to the window and watched the vanishing column. I imagined that the hunched form of a woman that I saw with a white string bag on her shoulder was my mother . . . Soon this also vanished.

So it was that with the piece of bread that I did manage to give her, my mother went straight to the jaws of death. She went like a hero, with a smile in her eyes so that, God forbid, I would not see in her fearful eyes that she still wanted to live. Certainly she deserved to live, having spent twenty years caring for my invalid father who later had become paralyzed. She had at the same time helped us tend our store and above all had raised a houseful of children and made decent human beings out of us. But she left without complaint, content to be sacrificed for me, and not even her plea to God to die in her own bed was granted. No, not only was it not granted, but it is possible that she was buried alive. I don't even know where her grave is.

I went up to my father. He saw how miserable I was, so he began to plague me with questioning eyes, since he was unable to speak and, using his hands, he asked me where Mama was. I told him that Mother had gone to another camp, and that as soon as he felt better, we would join her there. The next day Father again started to plague me, asking where Mother was—he wanted to see her. When would we be on our way to join her?

Meanwhile Yom Kippur of 1941 arrived. Before the fast there had been nothing to eat except for some tea and bits of bread. We fasted the day of Yom Kippur. Father felt very ill from fasting, so

Dr. Rosenblum asked me what I intended to do now with my father, whether he should be given an injection to keep him alive or be allowed to die. It was only a matter of an injection. I was devastated, uncertain as to what to do. I decided that Father should be given camphor in order to revive him a bit and to prolong his life. At the same time I wondered what sort of a life it was. Wait—one fine day the murderers would notice him and take him away to be shot. What kind of a life was that! But I thought, if my mother were here with me now at such a decisive moment of Father's life, what would she tell me to do? With such thoughts I stood beside my father and watched him begin, slowly, to breathe more easily. And when he came back to normal, I felt lighter in my heart and rejoiced that I would still have someone to care for; that I was not completely alone in the world. Possibly, had my father died then, I wouldn't be alive now myself, because my work at the hospital kept me from many dangers.

A few days later the ghetto was closed off from the city and we began to suffer from starvation. Until now, those who worked in the city were able to bring something into the ghetto—a bit of soup, a piece of bread. Now this ended; now everyone, I among them, felt the pangs of hunger. My father lay there starving. He would indicate to me, with tears in his eyes, that he was hungry, but I had to pretend I didn't notice. Once he suddenly got so angry at me for not giving him something to eat that I thought he would have hit me, had he been able to, though he had never hit me or any of his children in all his life. His look was enough. We got one kilo of bread per week, so I would cut the crust off for myself and the soft part I would divide up into portions for Father for the whole week, hiding it somewhere near his bed. I didn't let him see where the full ration was. The noon meal was old stale cabbage barely warmed, since there was no wood for cooking. In addition everyone got a liter of sour water. From the cabbage "soup," I would pick out the thick part and feed it spoon by spoon to my father; the watery remains I would drink myself. This was our whole "sustenance" in the ghetto. Naturally, from such "meals" we were not able to quiet our hunger. I was so faint from hunger that I couldn't stand, nor could Father lie peacefully in his bed.

Once I was in another room attending to a patient when I suddenly heard someone calling me from my father's room: "Pesia! Pesia!" Several voices kept calling me at the same time. I immediately understood that something had happened to Father and came running. When I reached Father's bed, I saw that he was choking on a piece of bread which he apparently had snuck from my hiding place. But since he had been in a rush to swallow the piece of bread so that I wouldn't catch him at the "theft," he had begun to choke and had asked the other patients to save him. The patients had become frightened and started to shout, calling for me because who else could they call? Frightened, but smiling, I took the too-large morsel from my father's mouth, and scolded him, "Father, have you become a thief already?"

He looked at me with guilty, exhausted, pleading eyes, asking me not to be angry with him. He indicated that he wanted me to move the bread further away from him because he couldn't help himself when hunger overtook him. I calmed him, laid him back in his bed, and returned miserably to my work. More than once Father would take his ration of bread in his mouth, choke, and ask me to help him. I would take the bread out of his mouth with my fingers and he would beg forgiveness with such childlike, pleading eyes that they follow me to this day and never leave me.

Meanwhile, hunger ate away at us. Every day people died from hunger. I felt that my days were numbered, so I took from my father's pillow a bracelet with three precious stones that I had kept hidden there. Through a middleman named Packerman, a tinsmith, I traded it for a pound of butter and a loaf of bread. My father's joy when I brought him the bread and butter was indescribable. He asked me to hide it under his pillow and he indicated to me that I shouldn't divide it among the sick, but keep it for the two of us. He knew that I didn't feel good eating when others were hungry.

But this time he watched me lest I give a crust to someone from our "treasure." When I would cut the single slice for us he would look me straight in the eyes and ask me to hide the bread again immediately. As long as the bread lasted things were bearable, but when I cut the last slice of bread Father's eyes became sad. "What will happen now?" he asked me with his hands. It tore at my heart. I could no longer take the sour water in my mouth. I began to vomit green bile from hunger.

In addition, it was a cold winter and we froze; many froze to death in their beds. Father indicated to me that he was bitterly cold. In the hospital there were only a few hot water bottles and I didn't know who to give them to first. I got around this dilemma by making sure that everyone got one for at least half an hour during the day, my father included. I covered him with my summer coat and would go about in the cold with only a summer dress with short sleeves, shivering so that my teeth chattered.

Slowly every source of bread vanished from the ghetto. Once I went into a room where a few rotten potatoes were being cooked. The smell of the potatoes nearly drove me insane. I felt that if someone were to give me a small piece of potato at that moment, they would save my life. But how could I ask for a piece of potato from strangers who were just as hungry as me? So I went back to the hospital and had a good cry. Frau Dunayevsky, another nurse in the sick block, saw me crying; she was very surprised because no one ever saw me crying. I was always on my rounds from one patient to the next, doing what I was told to do. Sometimes I did cry, but only at night, when I would go on my rounds among the sick, or when I was able to sneak away to the cemetery. Frau Dunayevsky begged me to tell her what happened, so I told her: I couldn't stand the hunger any longer. She understood me very well because she was just as hungry as I was. "When will our miseries be over?" she asked me.

However, I didn't want my father to see how troubled I was, because what kept him alive was my good spirits. I washed my face and went to him with a smile. He could sense, though, how miserable I was and that I was trying to trick him. I wanted to brush everything off, but my father didn't smile. He indicated to me that we were both equally hungry; he himself began to cry. Though he cried, he asked me not to cry. But how could I not cry when I saw Father dying of hunger and of cold? I promised him, though, that I wouldn't cry and I went to attend to my patients who had no one in their loneliness; they were all very fond of me because I never deserted them, neither by day nor by night.

I grew weaker from day to day and my face swelled up from hunger and the cold. One night I wanted to steal my father's bread—the portion that had been prepared for him for the following day. I went up to the bed but stood there: should I do it or not? I reached my hand toward the piece of bread but—I controlled myself. I hid the portion of bread even better so that I wouldn't catch sight of it and ran from the room as though I were escaping a fire. I busied myself with any kind of work, just so that the night would pass. I came less often into the room where my father lay. And so I was doubly grateful the following day when I could offer my father that same portion of bread without Father even beginning to know that I, his own daughter, had wanted to steal his last bit of bread.

As the days passed and the hunger ate away at us, my father became so thin that he no longer had any flesh on which to lie. Every five minutes I had to shift him to his other side. He stopped asking for me when he had to relieve himself and dirtied himself where he lay. I had to clean everything up, but I realized that it wouldn't be much longer that I would have to suffer with my father. Soon I would no longer have anyone to whom to give a piece of bread and a piece of sauerkraut. Soon I would be alone . . . From such thoughts I felt very wretched, because I so much did not want my sick father to leave me.

On February 19, 1942, the workers returned from the city very frightened; they all stayed in the ghetto overnight. We thought at that time that this was the end and began preparing for our last road, the one from which no one had ever yet returned. I went to sleep with my Aunt Musia that night; my face was so swollen that my eyes hardly showed. That evening, more than usual, the workers went around looking for relatives or people they were close to. One of them, Abrasha Zweigorn, greeted my aunt. My aunt told him that I was Pesia Frankel-Zaltzman. He took a good look at me, and when he saw what had become of me, one of his good friends, he started to cry bitterly. Because his wife, who had been shot, had been a good friend of my aunt, and because he himself had always been welcomed by our family, he promised that from that day forth he would help me and my father—provided that he were still allowed to go to the city to work. Abrasha gave me a piece of bread and I went off to share it with Father, and to tell him who gave it to me.

I noticed, however, that this time my father didn't express any pleasure over the piece of bread. I looked closer and saw that he was dying. Over the next few days he grew weaker and weaker. I could see that he wouldn't be suffering much longer, nor would I have to suffer much longer with him. I called over my good friend, Nurse Breen, and asked her to take a look at my father. "You must be prepared for this, which is best for him," she said to me. "For him death is much preferable to further suffering, and your own suffering. Now at least you can be sure that he won't be shot, but will die a natural death."

I still wanted to give him something. I ran into someone I knew, Glika Maggid, and I told her of my father's condition. She was lying languishing, but she took from somewhere her last spoonful of sugar and gave it to me for my father. But when I dissolved the bit of sugar in hot water and spooned it into my father's mouth, the sip of water stuck in his throat and he started to wheeze. From minute to minute life left him. That was Sunday night, Monday morning, February 23, the sixth day of the Hebrew month of Adar, two o'clock in the morning. I put my ear to his heart and asked him if he knew who was beside him. I told him it was me, his daughter Pesia. He embraced me with his last bit of strength. In half an hour he was gone. Till the last minute, I held his hand.

I sat beside his bed until six o'clock in the morning when some-one came into the hospital. I lost all my usual self-control as I sat there beside my dead father. I felt that now I was completely alone, so alone that it couldn't be worse. Finished. I had no one to fear for, and would suffer for no one. No one would any longer hear my father's sounds.

The doctors congratulated me at my "luck" at what had hap-pened: my father had died a natural death. He hadn't been shot. For eight months I had managed to keep my father from the hands of the murderers. At one o'clock the next morning, someone came to tell me that the grave was ready. I didn't have any shoes so I bor-rowed a pair of felt boots somewhere, grabbed a kerchief for my head and went down with Aunt Musia to see my father put to his eternal rest. When I realized that out of five sons there was none left to say Kaddish at their father's open grave, the pain was so great that I felt that my heart was tearing apart. But at the last minute my cousin Mendel Hellerman came and said Kaddish. Afterwards, the prayer "God who is full of mercy" was said and then it was over. That was how my father was relieved of his great suffering, and that was how the earth covered that which had been so dear to me and had given me courage for eight months to endure endless tribulation. I put a flask in the grave beside my father and in it I put a note with my father's name in Yiddish and in Russian. He was seventy-one years old.

When I came home from the funeral and lay down in the bar-rack on the three boards where I used to sleep beside my aunt Musia, Frau Strekovich, the good woman who had helped me pre-pare my father for burial, came over to me and handed me a hot cup of tea, sweetened, with a teaspoon. I realized that for eight months I hadn't seen a sweetened cup of tea, nor a teaspoon, and the tears started to choke me. With such thoughts I fell asleep. I slept through the whole night. There was no longer anyone to call me. I was left like the broken branch of a large lovely tree.

Chava Rosenfarb

꙳

CHAVA ROSENFARB BEGAN WRITING AT THE AGE OF EIGHT, encouraged by her father, who believed in her talent. A prolific and prominent Yiddish writer, Rosenfarb has produced short stories, novels, plays, essays, and poetry. Much of her work deals with the Holocaust. Born in 1923 in Lodz, Poland—an important industrial city before the Second World War—she studied at the local high school *(gymnasium)*. After the Nazi invasion of Poland in 1939, she was incarcerated in the Lodz ghetto, then relocated to Auschwitz and Bergen-Belsen. After liberation in 1945, she lived as a displaced person in Belgium before immigrating to Montreal in 1950. Her first collection of ghetto poems, *Di balade fun nekhtikn vald* [The Ballad of Yesterday's Forest] was published in 1947. Her work has been widely anthologized around the world and translated into English and Hebrew. She is the recipient of numerous awards, including the Helen and Stan Vine National Book Award in 2005 (for *Survivors: Seven Short Stories,* translated by Goldie Morgentaler), the Sholem Aleichem Prize from Israel in 1990, and the 1979 Manger Prize, Israel's highest literary honor. She also received the John Glassco Prize for Literary Translation in 2000 for her translation of her novels *Bociany* and *Of Lodz and Love.* Her major work, *The Tree of Life: A Trilogy of Life in the Lodz Ghetto*, translated along with Goldie Morgentaler, is being released in three volumes by the University of Wisconsin Press. She currently resides in Lethbridge, Alberta, where in June 2006 she received an honorary doctorate from the University of Lethbridge, the first such honor to be given a Yiddish writer in Canada.

Arguing with the Storm

Chava Rosenfarb's "Letters to God" *[Briv tsu got]* was published in 1995 in the quarterly journal *Di goldene keyt* [The Golden Chain]. While protagonist Dr. Yacov Sapir's present life is one of North American middle-class affluence, he is, like so many of Rosenfarb's characters, inhabited by his past as a Holocaust survivor.

Letters to God

❧

CHAVA ROSENFARB

Translated by Goldie Morgentaler

Lord, it is time. The summer has been very long . . .
Drive the last sweetness into the heavy wine . . .
Whoever has not yet found a home builds a home no more.
Whoever is now alone will remain so for a very long time
Will stay awake—will write long letters—

So WROTE THE POET RAINER MARIA RILKE IN "AUTUMN DAY," a letter in verse addressed to you, dear God. So many letters have been written to you, so many people crying out to you with so many words, expressing their longing in prayers, in sighs, and lamentations.

Why, then, do I regard my own writing to you as something tasteless and cynical? Is it because my summer has been devoid of the sweetness of heavy wine, or because I doubt your existence altogether? In my desolation and loneliness, I clutch at you despite my perception of your non-existence, so that you might, at least, serve me as a companion, as a comrade, or—forgive the thought—as a crutch.

I read somewhere of the publication of a book of letters to God written by children. And what am I after all? No more than a child—a child who has failed to learn how to write, a lost child with prematurely graying hair and a nervous heart, an adult child who still carries his immaturity around within him like a shield against life. Because it is false to think that You have created us in Your image. It is we who have created You in our image, Immature God. Maybe this is why You come into my mind, Great Absent One, whenever I think of fatherhood, whenever I think of my own father, or of myself as a father.

Tateshe, you are dying. I expire before the fact of your imminent desertion, right now, this very minute, even as you linger on your sickbed in the room on the other side of the corridor of my house.

I remember how you carried me on your shoulders when I was three years old. You twisted your head around to look up at me from between my small shoes. "How do you like riding on top of your father, my son?" you asked, laughing. You took me on outings to the amusement park. You held me on your lap, strapped us both into the seat of the carousel, and we flew round and round the globe. It was a familiar globe, embraced by your strong paternal arms. The word "loneliness" had not yet come into existence.

I also remember another day, Father, when you boarded the green streetcar with me, and we set out for the Green Market to buy raspberries which had just ripened on the bushes growing in the fields near the villages. I remember the raspberries' cheerful dark red color, their bittersweet taste, and I can still see in my memory your mustache spotted with grains of raspberry red as we sat in the tram on our way home, both of us picking raspberries from the basket and popping them into our mouths. The moment we entered the apartment, Mama smiled at us with her raspberry lips. She poured white cream from a white jug into the white bowl full of dark red raspberries and sprinkled white sugar on top, so that the raspberries became still sweeter, tastier, juicier, and redder beneath the cream.

I also remember the day, Father, when like an avenging God you spanked me—for having told a lie instead of confessing to playing hooky from school on that day in early spring when I skipped classes and went to the park to watch the ice breaking up on the lake.

I remember many other days with you, Father—the good days and bad days of my childhood—when you were like God to me, and both the bitter and the sweet days were happy ones. But what of that if I did not recognize them as such at the time?

You reproach me, Father, for not coming into your room often enough, for not sitting by your bed once in a while. "You cannot bear the sight of me . . . It's been taking too long, hasn't it?" your wise, faint smile seems to ask. You slide your pained watery eyes along my right arm, trying to ascertain whether I've come in just to be with you for a while, or whether I'm hiding the syringe with morphine behind my back to give an injection. You know as well as I do that the syringe is the head of a snake, and that its prick is the snake's sharp tongue injecting you with deadly poison.

Should I tell you that I so rarely enter your room to sit by your side because I am too afraid of your suffering? I am afraid that in a moment of despair I will fulfill your secret wish and put an end to your life—out of pity, out of my own painful helplessness. I avoid coming in, because I love you so much, and so childishly. It is the power of that love that chases me away from you. I am so attached to you, Father—*Tateshe!*—that the attachment feels like a rope wound tightly around my neck, choking me with such force that I feel I will lose my mind.

That is why I cling to you, you who know everything and

nothing. You are my anti-god, you who are so sick and helpless, you who are dying. That is why I cry out to you from the depths of my cursed confusion: Help me now that there is no help to be had.

I haven't got the faintest notion why you planted this idea in me of trying to "write" to you, the way Kafka wrote to his father, nor why I should feel the need to do so right now, from my bed, at this cold nightmarish hour before the dawn. Don't you know that my inability to hold a pen in my hand means that I am unable to bring to the surface of my mind all the emotions boiling inside me? That is your fault. Or God's fault. Because a father must be obeyed. It was He who wanted me to become a linguistic impotent. That is why I've never written anything. It just doesn't work. All the sluices have been slammed shut inside me—for life. I know that this does not matter to You, Eternal One; my literary lameness has no meaning *sub specie aeternitatis.* But to me it is of primary importance. To be an unfulfilled writer means to choke on one's soul as if it were a bone that cannot be swallowed.

Do you remember, Father, how you used to plan my future for me? According to your blueprint I was meant to become a famous scientist. I remember when I was eleven or twelve years old. We were on our way home from watching a soccer game in Polesie on the outskirts of town. You went from talking about the brilliant goalkeeper to speaking of a more important hero—me, the brilliant future benefactor of mankind. Yes, with dogged determination you tried to implant highly ethical ambitions in me. You encouraged and exhorted me; you overflowed with enthusiasm as you explained why knowledge is power. You told me about Kepler, about Newton, about Robert Fulton, about Edison, about Pierre and Marie Curie and, of course, about Albert Einstein. You lit one cigarette after another, puffing with enthusiasm, pushing your cap back so far on your forehead that it almost fell off. And so, keeping your other hand on my shoulder, you talked to me.

"Remember, Yankeleh my son," you went on solemnly as the

cigarette smoke spiraling out of your mouth linked one word to the next. "If you're struck by an interesting idea, write it down. If you come across a clever thought in a book, copy it immediately. You never know from where a sudden spark of inspiration might come."

"But Papa," I tried to argue. "I want to become a writer, a poet, not a scientist."

"Of course," you patted my shoulder affectionately. "Becoming a scientist will make you a writer or a poet. The sciences are full of poetry. They penetrate the secrets of life and discover the basis of existence, they resonate with the music of the spheres, pointing towards the mystery of the beyond and towards a symbiosis with God Himself. It is not a coincidence that Albert Einstein is a first-rate violinist."

So we walked along the paths of the suburban fields, engaged in this dreamlike argument, until, suddenly, a gang of hooligans appeared from behind a cottage and began pelting us with stones. A stone struck my forehead and immediately raised a bump. I still have that bump. It has grown into my brain. No wonder that I carry no *tselem elokhim,* no image of God, on my forehead, but bear instead the mark of human hatred. Later I learned that those whom the Germans did not permit to join the army, either for political reasons or because they were schlemiels, were called *Waffen-unfähig,* which meant they were unfit to bear arms. As for me, until I entered the concentration camp I was *Lebens-unfähig,* unfit for life. Perhaps it is this shortcoming of mine that has attached me so powerfully to you, Father.

So powerfully attached to you was I that in order to spite you, when I reached my majority I insisted on becoming a poet and not a scientist.

"Knowledge is not power, but weakness," I argued. "Science knows nothing. Poetry knows all." This was how I explained my philosophy of life to you.

I liked to play with words. I derived great pleasure from the sounds produced by certain conjunctions of syllables and by the rhythmic harmony of certain lines when they were juxtaposed. And so I brought myself up on poetry, playing father to my own self. I grew up on literature. I sought refuge in literature from you and from your power over me, from your inescapable godliness. I ran to literature to escape my fear of life, my fear of the gentiles. I lived more within the confines of books than in the real world.

I remember there was one particular day when I realized for the first time how liberating writing was. This happened on the morning when my high school teacher asked us to write a composition in class. "Walks with my Father" was the title of what I was supposed to write. Up to then my walks with you had been casual and leisurely, of no particular significance. But this very informality assumed an astonishing dimension once I set about transforming it into a literary text. Nothing came of the composition. I did not write it, because as soon as you entered my mind, I—pen in hand—made a broad clumsy gesture over the white sheet of paper and knocked over the inkstand. The black ink spilled all over the white sheet of paper and the teacher threw me out of the classroom. Ever since then I have been an outcast, an outsider in the world of those who are able to manage with words. I grew up a frustrated writer.

We were wonderful comrades in those days, Father. And yet, during those first years of my manhood, I imperceptibly began to despise you, to hate you with a profound hatred for the sin of being imperfect. I could not forgive your weaknesses. I labeled them hypocrisy, two-facedness, narrow-mindedness. I believed that despite your liberal outlook on life and your lofty preaching about knowledge and science, you remained intellectually undeveloped, that your intolerance of me matured along with my own physical and mental ripening. You made no effort to understand me. You did not even attempt, you were not even curious to see the world through my eyes. I could not abide your dry practicality, your desire to clip my wings, your habit of disparaging my dreams. I could not accept the pettiness of your authority.

Moreover, you were the king who begrudged me my privileged position in the heart of the queen, my mother, whose crown prince I was. I was the light of her eyes—as she was of mine. With your insistent practicality, you brought us both down to earth and kept us there; you trampled on the joy that existed between her and me. I could hardly bear the sight of you.

How ridiculous all this seems to me now, *Tateshe,* how senseless and silly. All resentment has been annulled before the gigantic shadow spreading its black wings over my world. I cannot find the slightest speck of meaning in the dazzling darkness that threatens to blind me as it descends upon us. During those green hopeful years, when you accompanied me through life, it was easy for me to invent a purpose for myself, a destiny—whether in agreement with you or in opposition to you—and to cling to the illusion that my existence in this world had significance. Even in the concentration camp, I clung to this belief. But now, after so many golden, post-liberation autumns have passed, now, as you lie on your sickbed in the next room as if it were a raft about to depart, while the rope that binds me to you slips from my hand, I feel hollow inside, empty throughout my whole being. The fear of your suffering, Father, is the only proof I have left that I am alive.

Which brings me finally to the truth about myself—that I have become incurably psychotic. The psychotic paranoia of a schizophrenic personality is my diagnosis, formulated primarily by my wife Malka.

I am shaking. I am attacked by spasms of terror that at any moment the door will burst open and the Doctor of the Universe, my wife Malka, will make her appearance. She will pierce me with her burning and caressing green eyes and encircle me with the pitch-black strands of her silken hair. She will gather me into the embrace of her smooth, plump, steel-like arms which are so deceptively tender. I worship her. She is all that I have. She is my destiny, and there is no help for it.

Daylight is turning the sky gray. The first rays of sunshine have dappled the windowpane. I can see Malka approaching. She plants herself beside me and I can hear her say, "Good morning, my treasure. I am going to give you an injection, so that you will not feel the electric shocks. Today is Friday. The electroshock therapy will bring you a peaceful Sabbath."

She ties the sleeves of my straitjacket and straps me in with the silk of her endlessly long black hair. She grips my shoulders with her soft hands, which have the power of pliers, and the loving eyes of her lovely face pierce me with the desire to destroy. She brings a deadly cure with her electroshocks. The electrodes press against my temples, my head is ringed with straps. She touches the switch. Save me, Father, save me!

*

Dr. Yacov Sapir woke with a scream and sat up on his bed. His wife Malka, who slept beside him, also sat up with a start.

"What happened?" she asked.

Yacov fell back onto the pillow and emitted a deep sigh of relief. He rubbed his forehead with both hands.

"Nothing . . . Nothing at all, sweetheart. I dreamed something, although I had the impression that I was awake. A nightmare. I dreamed that I was one of my patients." He stared at her absently for a while, as if he did not recognize her. Then he took her hand and laid it on his chest. Her face seemed to be floating above him. He looked up at her and smiled sadly. "You were in the dream too, my dearest. Your eyes were green instead of black." He caressed her fingers tenderly as her hand slowly crept over his hairy chest. "How is he doing?" he asked. "He's slept through the whole night, hasn't he?"

"He's still asleep," she whispered back. "After the injection you gave him last night . . ."

"As long as he's not in pain."

"I know. I also feel better when he's asleep. As soon as I hear him moaning I'm ready to run to the other end of the house."

Yacov searched the dark warmth of her eyes for a ray of encouragement to help him face the oncoming day. The black silken strands of her hair were scattered, Medusa-like, over the bright skin of her neck and shoulders; they lay entangled in the shoulder straps of her nightgown, tempting his lips to a touch. For a moment he imagined himself gathering her passionately into his arms. Instead, he only gave her a quick peck on the cheek and got out of bed.

As soon as he emerged into the corridor his youngest son, Sammy, barefoot and half-naked, came running out to greet him. Grabbing hold of his father's knees, the four-year-old exclaimed in his ringing little voice, "Papa, I love you!"

Yacov gathered his son into his arms, then, raising him onto his shoulders, hopped around the corridor with him. He looked up from between the child's bare feet and repeated the question that his own father had used to ask him: "How do you like riding on top of your father, my son?"

He glanced quickly down the corridor at the closed door of the sickroom, then turned back.

Half an hour later he was dressed in the skin of Dr. Yacov Sapir, wearing his workday outfit of spotless white shirt, brown tie, and freshly ironed brown jacket and slacks. The shiny brown tips of his freshly polished shoes peeked out from beneath the cuffs of his slacks. He sat at the breakfast table in the kitchen hurriedly gulping down his cereal and milk. At his side sat Malka in her carelessly buttoned pink housecoat. Sammy sat on her lap, trying to construct something out of the teaspoons on the table. The spoons clinked loudly between his plump fingers. The other children had already left for school.

"You'll have to increase the dosage today," Malka said to Yacov as he wolfed down the spoonfuls of cereal. The grains cracked unpleasantly between his teeth. He was trapped in the same desperate tension that had not lifted since the day he had brought his father home from the hospital. "I thought I heard him groan a few times at dawn," Malka continued. "I know that you're pleased to have brought him home from the hospital, but, if you want to know my opinion . . . "

Yacov had a vague sense that he was beginning to be afraid of her. Perhaps this was merely an aftertaste of his horrible dream of the night before. He pretended not to hear what she said and buried his face deeper in the bowl of cereal, eating faster. He sensed that she was waiting for an answer and eventually felt himself obliged to speak.

"They refused to keep him any longer. You know this."

She nodded. "Of course. It made no sense. There's nothing they can do for him anyway."

It seemed to him that he had to appease Malka, as if she were a lioness ready to pounce. Any moment now he would put his arms around her and close her mouth with his lips. He softly stroked her arm, as if to console her.

"You are an angel, my love, to have agreed to it. You have no idea how grateful I am to you. I don't know how I would have managed without you. The children are taking his presence in the house better than I thought they would, don't you agree?"

"Yes, it might seem so on the surface."

Sammy clinked the teaspoons more loudly to keep up with the emphatic conversation he was having with himself. Malka continued in a whisper: "But what impact it's really having on them is hard to know. Even if they forget his presence, it doesn't necessarily mean that their subconscious doesn't register the atmosphere in the house."

"What's wrong with the atmosphere in the house?" Yacov asked, barely able to control his annoyance. "Aren't we carrying on with our normal routine?"

"How can you say such a thing? How can you speak about any kind of normalcy at all?"

"Perhaps you're right."

"Of course I'm right. The door of the sickroom is closed shut, but on the other side of that door it is deadly quiet . . . The whole thing horrifies me. I don't know how much longer I'll be able to bear it. I still think that it would have been much wiser to place him in the palliative care unit."

"Understand . . ." Yacov's voice caught in his throat and he coughed. He pushed away the bowl of unfinished cereal. "I cannot do it. I must not. He wants it this way."

"Which way? He hasn't got the faintest idea of what's happening to him."

"He knows and so do I."

"But you don't have to obey him. You're not a child."

"He's my father."

"And he's still a despot."

"Don't talk like that."

"I'm sorry. But you'll inject him with a larger dose today, won't you?"

"Say something pleasant to me, Malka."

"I love you. Do it for me, Yacov, for the sake of my nerves. When he's asleep I feel calmer."

Yacov turned his head towards the window as if he were seeking an escape from the discomfort within him. A sumptuous maple tree with a wealth of leaves spread its regal branches over the entire backyard, as if it were a dappled umbrella. The branches of the tree pressed against the kitchen window with the autumnal brightness of gold and red leaves—a cheerful announcement of decay—and blurred Yacov's view. The dull pain in his heart overwhelmed him.

"Autumn in full splendor," he motioned with false cheer in the direction of the bright outdoors. "At least you, Malka, ought to be enjoying these last sunny days. Take Sammy and go to the park as soon as the nurse arrives. I have to hurry." He stood up, took both of Malka's hands in his, and made her stand too. He pulled her towards his chest. "Look at that autumn splendor outside. Just look at that tree."

They both observed the tree longingly, until it seemed to Yacov that the black of Malka's eyes was swimming towards the tree on tearful drops of sorrow. He was grateful to her for participating so deeply in his suffering. He embraced her more forcefully and desperately kissed her lips, as though determined to inhale hope from her mouth, or as if he were afraid that as soon as he removed his lips from hers she would open her mouth to plead with him, or to insist that he . . .

Hastily he detached himself from her. "I have a hard day at the hospital," he said quickly.

She followed him into the corridor. "Don't come home late, please. I dread having to stay here alone all day. And give him the injection before you leave. Please, don't forget."

He nodded and entered his office to prepare the injection for his father.

Days passed and the scene in the kitchen was repeated every morning. This morning, too, Malka sat by Yacov's side at the breakfast table, while Sammy played on the floor. Yacov gulped down his breakfast cereal, trying to dull his private pain by concentrating on the public anguish reflected in the headlines that caught his eye from the front page of the newspaper. Now and then he raised his head and looked around. Sammy sat on the floor next to Malka's bare feet. A red velvet slipper dangled carelessly from her toe. The autumn sunlight shimmered through the entanglement of gold and red maple leaves and fell on Sammy's brown ringlets and on the shiny silk of Malka's black hair.

Yacov felt Malka's insistent eyes and glanced up from the paper. An expression of sadness and pain was etched into the net of fine thin wrinkles on her face. He realized how poorly she looked. Her face seemed not to belong to the rest of her body, which radiated an attractive feminine warmth and freshness, even now, as she sat with her disheveled hair spread in all directions over her carelessly buttoned pink housecoat. Without cosmetics, without powder, rouge, or lipstick, her face took on a pale yellow cast which seemed to change the color of her eyes from black to green. The deep furrows around her eyes and mouth pricked at his heart like the thin needles of a syringe. They seemed to inject a poisonous guilt into his bloodstream.

She put her hand on his knee. He covered her hand with his and they looked at each other silently. A multitude of inexpressible thoughts and feelings traveled between them. Then she moved her lips and he grew frightened at what she was going to say. He quickly covered her mouth with his hand.

"Hush, don't say a thing," he muttered. "Don't think that I don't know how unjust it is that I am away from home all day long while you carry the burden of this all alone. But, after all, he doesn't take up much of your time, and . . ."

"And what else, my dearest?"

"The nurse does everything necessary."

"That makes no difference. It is the atmosphere in the house, the fear, the . . . I don't know myself what to call it."

"I know what you mean."

"The children will be home from school very early today. It will be hard. Give him a larger dose."

"Why? He's asleep all the time as it is, for quite a few days now."

"Yes, but he wakes occasionally. I beg you."

"I mustn't."

"A slightly larger dose. Do it for me, dearest."

"He won't be able to take it."

Sammy jumped to his feet and ran out of the kitchen as if he sensed the nature of his parents' secrets. Malka seated herself on Yacov's lap. He stroked the long black hair which flowed over her shoulders, highlighting by contrast her pale, anxious face. The morning sun cut like a narrow surgical scalpel into the pink housecoat which lay against her breast. She caressed his head and sighed as she whispered into his graying hair: "The sight of that closed door terrifies me. It tears my heart apart. I am ashamed to smile at the children."

There was a knock at the front door. Yacov straightened himself with a start.

"It's the mailman," Malka said in a tone meant to calm him.

She stood up and straightened her housecoat. She made this movement in graceful innocence, ignorant of its enticing effect. Yacov was startled. He recognized in her the witch he had seen in a dream not long before. Suddenly he realized how much he hated her. He could scarcely breathe in her presence. He was afraid of her, afraid of what he felt. No! It was impossible! This must not happen! He must love her! She was the only light in his life. He must not run away from her. She supported him with her love, so devotedly, so magnificently. How could he be so brutal, so ungrateful?

He went out to the mailbox and returned carrying a pile of letters in his hand, with which he entered his office. He opened the letters, but did not read them. They did not interest him. He was thinking of Malka and looked about him as if he were looking for her. He remembered how much she liked his office. His father had liked it too.

The walls of his office were specially insulated, so as to prevent any external sound from entering the room, which was divided by an oriental screen. On the far side stood a comfortable black leather sofa, with a matching black leather armchair and footstool nearby. Four evenings a week he conducted here his fifty-minute therapy sessions with his patients. On one side of the divider stood his mahogany desk, flanked on either side by two bookcases which stood against the walls. Nearby stood the locked glass cabinet with glass shelves upon which were arranged various medicines, including a small bottle of morphine.

From the very beginning Yacov had disliked the elegance of this room. It did not really suit his taste. But he had decorated it this way for the sake of his patients, since this was the style of the times. It conformed to the business side of his profession. This was the decor that his father and Malka had argued for when they assisted him in setting up his office. Actually his father never insisted, but merely suggested what his son should do. He gave no orders to an adult son with a medical diploma; he was merely thinking aloud. So too Malka; she was only thinking aloud.

Yacov unlocked the door of the cabinet and prepared the injection for his father.

There was an unpleasant acrid smell in the sickroom. The nurse who daily washed the bedsores on the sick man's body applied to them a soothing cream that left a heavy medicinal smell in the room. Yacov was used to the smell. He never minded it at the hospital, but here, in his father's room, he could hardly bear it.

"I have no relation to the man lying here on this bed. He's just another one of my patients, that's all," Yacov told himself, trying to believe in his self-imposed indifference. In fact, there was no resemblance between the face he saw before him and the familiar face of his father. And yet the face was so familiar, so intimate, as if he himself were lying prostrate on the bed.

The sick man snored heavily. With careful movements, so as to avoid waking his father, Yacov removed the blanket that covered the sick man's body, revealing the yellowish, pyjama-clad torso that lay as flat against the bedsheet as if it were a two-dimensional cardboard cut-out. The wheezing snore seemed to be coming from somewhere deep inside the body. Yacov had the impression that he was snoring along with his father, that he had joined him on this voyage.

Suddenly, he felt an enormous desire to see his father's eyes open, to see his mouth move, to hear words issue from between the cracked brownish lips. It had been many days since his father had been able to keep his eyes open, or had uttered anything resembling a word. Yacov rolled up the sleeve that covered his father's arm and quickly jabbed the needle into the loose flesh. The body on the bed did not react, and yet the entire room was suddenly invaded by a stifling heat that buzzed with hissing, sizzling, never expressed, painful words.

Yacov's knees buckled. He sank into the chair beside the bed and allowed his eyes to rest on his father's scorched brown mouth, the source of the rasping, of the struggling breath—the only remaining sign of life.

*

It seems to me, Father, that we are still in the concentration camp. I remember our relief that we had both survived the horrifying trial of the first selection. Now I see you going alone to the last selection—the one which awaits me too somewhere, sometime, at some future date. Of course there is a moral difference between a selection based on the brutal movement of a human being's hand, and the selection conducted by a faceless fate. But the horror is the same, *Tateshe,* my brother in fate!

I see the two of us in the camp and I recall how our roles changed. I began to act the father to you, and in the process became your consoler and your consolation. In the camp it was impossible to argue with a treasure so miraculously saved as one's own flesh-and-blood father. We clung to each other. We nursed each other's wounds. We shared every crumb of food.

I remember how during the long marches in the winter, I carried you on my back and shoulders like Jesus carried his cross to Golgotha. And that was how I got you across the river, followed by a spray of bullets. In this way, we escaped from the camp a day before the liberation. It was then that I repaid you, Father, for giving life to me.

How painful it is to recall our happiness after the liberation. It consisted of more than the mere fact that we were no longer hungry and more than the simple fact that we were free; or that we could finally indulge our own painful memories, or argue freely about anything in the world, but mainly about politics. It consisted of an inexpressible sense of elation, as if the coming of the Messiah were at hand, an elation which, unfortunately, gradually evaporated—at least as far as I was concerned. Because you began again to cling to your pre-war ideology about the potential for human redemption, whereas I refused to hear such hogwash. I, the former dreamer, had sobered up for good—or so I thought. In truth, I began to see myself as suspended in a void—and, just as in pre-war times, I waited in vain for the salvation of poetry, of a new kind of poetry, to open the dams of unshed hopeful tears and bring about my redemption.

I recall how your salvaged life demanded, in time, that it should be lived, and you suddenly grew jealous of my youth. Here I look at you, Father, and I can hardly believe that you are the same man who was then so spring-like, had so much virility, and craved so actively the bodies of my young girlfriends. You used to steal the letters that I received from my fiancée Malka in order to read them in secret. In your love for me you acted with the greed of King Saul who had grown afraid of the young David—while I began to feel that you had become a burden and an obstacle to me.

Our campmates who had survived the war envied me for having saved my father, while I burned with shame that your devotion to me caused me discomfort. I was annoyed by everything you said. Every remark you made grated on my ears, driving me to the edge of distraction, just as Malka's words today irritated and exasperated me, making me feel two times, three times, a thousand times more disgusted with myself. I feel like a villain, like a Nazi.

Forgive my tears, *Tateshe*. This is the only place where I can weep freely. I can see you carrying me on your shoulders towards that day when I will be lying on such a bed as you are now—while my son Sammy says similarly distracted and distraught words of goodbye to me wordlessly in his mind.

I remember how triumphant you were, Father, when I decided to give in to you and become practical. I embarked on the study of medicine. How proud you were when I received my medical diploma! You even accepted with good cheer my specializing in psychiatry. That was my compromise choice. I told myself that psychiatry, like poetry, tackles the mystery of the human soul and heals its wounds in its own way. I deluded myself with the thought that I would be capable of alleviating the pain in the hearts of my former campmates, and I pretended ignorance of the fact that for the experiences of the camps there is no therapy, not even the passing of years.

You lived with my projects, Father; you identified with me. Thanks to me you imagined that you had finally lost your sense of alienation as an immigrant and become a co-participant in the strange tempo of life in America. Whenever you felt the urge to tease me a little, you—who could barely pronounce correctly a single English word—jokingly called me "Mister Shrink." To my ears this epithet, coming from your lips, sounded not like affectionate joking, but rather like a dismissive curse. "Mister Shrink!" It seemed to me that what you were really saying was: "Don't grow so far beyond me, don't efface me so completely!"

Until this very day you have a weakness for Malka, Father. You love her. I know it. The harmony between the two of you used to both please and irritate me. You both took delight in my achievements, you boasting of your gifted son and she of her gifted husband. Together you worried about my working so hard, and together you made me feel eternally in your debt.

In debt? Here you are lying, your life dimming, ebbing away, my dear *Tateshe,* and I can do nothing for you—except to kiss your limp hand, except to avenge myself on you for the sin of having loved me with such devotion, except to liberate you from your suffering and curse myself for it—as your beloved Malka's pleading eyes demand. (Or does it only seem so to me?) Oh, God, how I hate her—and myself. How can a person, especially someone who was an inmate of a concentration camp, flirt with such thoughts?

*

Yacov barely knew how he managed to steer the car through the traffic in the center of town as he drove to work. At the hospital, he forced himself to act normally, a normality that required so much effort and concentration that he felt as if he had been hypnotized.

After work he could not bring himself to go home. Instead, he went for a stroll in the park. The trees displayed the full splendor of Indian summer; each was a brown, red, orange, and yellow bouquet of color basking in the sunshine. Falling leaves floated like flakes of gold in the air and soundlessly fell upon the ground around the trunks of the trees. The paths and the grass were littered with piles of leaves, which crackled pleasantly under every step. Solitary bright leaves danced in the air, swaying on the arms of a light-footed breeze.

Yacov caught sight of the bright outfit of a young kindergarten teacher on an outing with her young charges. He approached the class and observed the youngsters burying themselves in the mountains of leaves, rolling with squeals of delight over the colorful heaps or skipping around them. The blond teacher gathered armfuls of leaves and laughingly allowed them to fall over the heads of the children. Golden leaves stuck to the wool of her sweater and caught in her hair, where they sparkled like pieces of jewelry.

Yacov moved still closer to the group of children. The teacher stared at him with her blue eyes dilated in surprise and apprehension. He bent down, picked up a pile of leaves, and, copying the teacher's movements, sprinkled the leaves over the children's heads.

"A golden rain of leaves," he said to her. And in order to relieve her anxiety, he introduced himself as a doctor employed at the neighboring hospital. He felt foolish, yet at the same time he was overcome by a feeling of playful intoxication. "Such a bright radiant world!" he exclaimed.

The blond teacher had obviously decided that the stranger posed no threat; her blue eyes cleared, and she smiled back at him. He noticed the sparkle of her two rows of white teeth. The sight of them dazzled him. He was convinced that he was dreaming, because only in a dream could everything around him appear so luminous. And in the midst of that luminosity shimmered the brilliance of the teacher's two rows of white teeth, like two rows of tiny light bulbs lit by the sun.

As if in a trance, he began to recite Rilke's "Autumn Day" to her:

Lord, it is time. The summer has been very long.
Spread your shadow over the sundials
and let loose the winds over the plains.

"How beautiful!" the young teacher sighed when he had finished. The sigh was a sad, dreamy exhalation, as if he had enchanted her.

"My father is dying." He was surprised to hear himself proclaim this, as if the news were an additional line to the poem he had just recited.

The light from the young teacher's teeth was extinguished behind the pursing of her narrow lips. She looked at him with compassion, "Oh, I'm so very sorry . . ." She whispered this with sincere regret.

"Do you love your father?" he asked her as one asks in a dream.

She shrugged her shoulders, "I have no father."

"What do you mean? How old were you when you lost him?"

"I never knew my father, never saw him with my eyes. He abandoned my mother when she was pregnant with me."

"Then you don't know what it means to have a father; and you don't know what it means to lose one," he said, as if to himself. "And you don't know the guilt, trailing after you like a heavy weight."

"Why guilt?"

"For having sinful thoughts."

He felt himself incapable of absorbing the entire picture of the young woman with the children against the background of the golden garden. Yet he felt love streaming into all his limbs. A tender love of spring, of youth, in the very middle of autumn. There was such a healing wisdom in life.

He felt a sting as he thought of Malka.

It was about nine o'clock in the morning. A gray autumnal morning, there was no sunshine. Yacov left his breakfast unfinished and left the kitchen. For a while he listened to the children chattering with Malka at the breakfast table. It was a holiday. Thanksgiving. Yacov had no consultations that day, nor did he go to the hospital.

"No school today!" the children's joyful exclamations echoed in his ears.

"No school today!" he murmured to himself as he entered his office. He glanced at the other side of the screen. How gladly would he stretch himself out on the couch, right now, this very Thanksgiving morning, and make a confession before someone, before some non-existent psychiatrist. But this he could not allow himself to do! He must not confess to anybody, not even to himself—because there was something he must do now, despite his cowardice, despite the horror that engulfed him—he must do it . . . He must!

He was aware that a day more steeped in darkness than today would most likely never again occur in his life. The stifling darkness in his mind sank deeper and deeper into his body, into his limbs. But just as a cloud descending into a valley leaves behind a mountain peak basking in light, so from somewhere above him a thin ray of brightness forced its way through: the image of the kindergarten teacher with the children. The image established a relationship between light and darkness. He saw himself in the camp, saw himself wearing an SS man's uniform over the striped rags of an inmate's clothing. From the other side of the fence Malka smiled consolingly, imploringly, promising, "Soon you will be free."

"Free? Idiot!" His face contracted with pain. "This is the moment when I really put on my chains."

His loneliness howled so desolately within him that he had to rush back into the kitchen in order to glance at his children and fortify himself with the sight of them, at least for a moment. There they were, sitting on the kitchen floor, playing dominoes. At the table sat Malka in her housecoat, her hair disheveled. Her glistening face looked sticky. Her tired eyes looked out at the maple tree which stared back through the gray window panes. Without sunshine on it, the maple tree looked pale, less significant. As soon as Yacov entered the kitchen, Malka transferred her gaze to him.

"Get dressed and go down into the park with the children," he told her calmly. He looked at her intently. Did she understand? She did. Her eyes caressed him tenderly. She stood up from the table, with what seemed to him an ugly smile of gratitude lighting up the corners of her mouth. He would never forgive her for this. He felt his fear . . . his hatred. She was the snake. She sat inside him like a dybbuk, entangling him in the nets of her poisonous medusa hair.

He drew near her, put his arm tenderly around her, and felt the warmth of her loose breasts through the thin fabric of her housecoat. "I love you, Malka, remember that," he whispered. He bent down to the children and a longing overcame him to stretch himself out on the floor beside them.

"Papa! Papa!" Sammy clasped him by the sleeve. "Let me ride on you a teeny-weeny bit!"

Malka went to get dressed. Yacov hopped round and round the kitchen table with Sammy on his shoulders. Soon Malka was back, carrying the children's clothing. With determined haste, she and Yacov dressed the children, after which she ushered them out of the house, closing the door behind her.

The house sank into frightful stillness. Yacov went back into his office, unlocked the cupboard with the medicines, and removed the small bottle of morphine and the syringe from the shelf. He prepared a package of cotton and started to fill the syringe, dipping the needle in the bottle. The glass tube of the syringe sucked in one centiliter after another. Slowly the fluid jumped the indicator lines on the glass, moving ever higher. For the last few weeks those lines had become the ladder that his fluttering heart had climbed towards the precipice of the present moment. His father's astonishingly strong heart had behaved normally for the past ten days, but four days ago the pulse had begun to show certain signs . . . The heart was starting to acknowledge the losing battle, it was beginning to surrender.

A strong heart is a matter of heredity. A strong heart is the heart of a giant. Yacov heard his own heart hammering against the walls of his veins, hammering in his temples. A huge heart beat inside the room, taking up the space of the entire world, dulling the senses. It pounded in Yacov's steps as he left the office and opened the door of his father's room.

The bed. Yacov's eyes take in the sight of it, along with the barely visible elevation in the middle of the blanket. His eyes travel along every fold in the blanket and finally up to the pillow where the head is resting. The head is strangely bare and round, a pair of gray hairs protrude from the scalp. The color of the skin mixes with the gray light from the windowpanes; the face is like a yellow autumn leaf. The eyes are shut. Good that they are shut. The dark-brown mouth is the only living point. It rasps. It rattles. It fights for a breath of air.

The arm rests limply on top of the blanket. Blood of my blood, flesh of my flesh. Father's sickbed is suspended in space like a hammock. In the hammock lies a little boy of three, and his father is swinging him back and forth.

A boyish voice cries: "Papa . . . Forgive me for the estrangement between us. Forgive me for the closeness . . . Forgive me for having to be your liberator . . . Forgive me for the sins which cannot be forgiven. Here am I, your son Yacov, watching with my eyes open—as I pierce your skin with the needle for the last time. I can see liberation trickling into your body while your illness trickles into me drop after drop. Jews take leave of each other with the blessing, 'Be well, go in good health, come back in good health.' Not *us*, Papa, not *us*. We don't take leave of each other. I am frightened. God, I am calling you from the depths of despair . . . I, your son Cain. I, your murderer who loves you, Papa."

He clasped the wrist of his father's hand in his. The pulse was gone. He kissed the hand, which was still hot with the life that was no more. It seemed to him that Sammy had thrown his little arms around Yacov's stiff legs. "I love you, Papa."

Rikuda Potash

＄

THE AUTHOR OF POETRY, SHORT STORIES, NOVELLAS, AND PLAYS, Rikuda Potash gained recognition within her lifetime from readers as well as her contemporaries in the literary and artistic community. Potash was born in Tshenstochov, Poland, in 1906, to a well-off, cultured family, and raised in Skale-Bayvidov. Although she began writing poetry in Polish as a young woman, she was radicalized by the anti-Semitic events of the time, particularly the Lemberg pogrom of 1918, in which at least seventy Jewish civilians were killed. Potash then began to study Yiddish literature and embraced Yiddish in her own writing. In 1924, she moved to Lodz and became active in the literary community, publishing her first poems in Yiddish. She married Yiddish poet Chaim Leib Fuks, and they had a daughter, Aviva. When the marriage ended in 1934, Potash moved with her daughter to Palestine; she published her first volume of poetry, *Vint oyf klavishn* [Wind on Keyboard] in the same year. Potash worked for over thirty years as the librarian of the Bezalel Art School and Museum in Jerusalem. She was influenced by and influenced the artistic scene in the city, particularly Mordecai Ardon, the renowned painter and director of the Bezalel. She often accompanied her pages of poetry with drawings, an expression of her preoccupation with issues of voice and vision. Her writing was acclaimed both in Israel and the United States for its eloquence, psychological insight, and cultural pluralism. She visited New York to attend a tribute in her honor shortly before her death in 1965.

Rikuda Potash's "The Sad House in Talbiye" [*Dos troyerike hoyz in Talbiye]* and "Rumiya and the Shofar" *[Rumiya un der shoyfer]* were published in the 1968 short story collection *In geslekh fun Yerushalayim* [In the Alleys of Jerusalem]. Both stories are set in Jerusalem. The troubled characters of "The Sad House in Talbiye" live lives that threaten to "go dark," depleted not only by the after-effects of the Holocaust, but as a consequence of the psychological toll of an embattled Israel. In "Rumiya and the Shofar," on the other hand, the spirit of the Sephardic washerwoman seems particularly resilient. Despite her marginalized position as a member of the minority Sephardic population, Rumiya possesses a sturdy sense of self. Shrugging off the condescension and conservatism of her Ashkenazi employer, as well as the prohibition against women blowing the shofar, Rumiya persists in her dreams.

The Sad House in Talbiye

∽

RIKUDA POTASH

Translated by Chana Thau

THE HOUSE WAS HIDDEN AMONG PINE TREES. IF IT WEREN'T for the smell of chloroform surrounding it, you'd have thought it a rest home. Nurse Monica sat on a bench outside. The sun was so low in the sky that it touched her red-gold hair. Wherever the sun went, it took laughter with it.

Monica, the nurse who worked afternoons, sat thinking she herself might be taken for one of the unfortunate patients. Her relatives in Mexico had written her, inviting her to take a holiday abroad in June, for which they promised to send her the money . . .

Monica, a pale, dreamy woman, looked at her hands, which now seemed to her like two withered leaves on a diseased tree. She looked at her legs, which were even thinner than they used to be. She was ashamed of her own thoughts. What lay heaviest on her heart was the young couple who were back for a third time. They'd given up all hope. She remembered the first time Mina, a beautiful blond, had come to the hospital with a nervous breakdown. Her neuroses were preventing her from becoming a sculptor, so she had fallen into a depression. She would stand for hours at the window, looking expressionlessly in one direction. Monica knew that Mina had genuine talent. But somehow a worm was burrowing through the beautiful apple. Monica found it easy to believe that one day she herself would belong to the population of the ill who stayed months, or years, in the sad house in Talbiye.

In the last days of autumn her thoughts spread like filaments through her mind. Sometimes she didn't know why she had chosen such an awful profession. She'd studied biology. Stopped in the middle. Thrown herself into psychology and, again, changed over—to nursing. Then Dr. Asasian had turned up. He'd persuaded her to work with him—here, where life was so different from everyday life on the outside. She no longer had the strength to escape this sad house. Dr. Asasian probably wouldn't even notice when, suddenly, she became one of his patients—then there would be no more plans for her, not about holidays in Mexico, nor with her relatives.

The sun suddenly turned into an immense ball of fire. Monica looked on despairingly as the sun blazed; no one realized that she might be scorched by it. In the garden, a bird's song woke Monica from her daydream; the bird began to warble an elegy on the sorrow of birds. She knew that bird. It had strange reddish-yellow feathers and a green skullcap on its head.

Monica went wearily into the white hallway. Standing there leaning against the east wall was Duvdivani, a tall, blond, green-eyed young man. He was talking to himself. Monica lay her pale, small hand on his shoulder and, with a forced smile, asked, "Did you see how red the sunset was?"

"The sun went and burned her house down," Duvdivani answered, twisting an unruly lock of hair.

"Why would she burn her own house down? Where would she go if her house burned down?"

"The sun's like Mina. Mina burned down her house too. So did I."

"I hate it when you talk nonsense, Duvdivani," Nurse Monica

smiled. "Sit down here on the bench with me. Mina will probably be coming soon. She's seeing Dr. Asasian now. He'll help her get better soon, so she can go back and learn to be an artist."

Duvdivani sat on a bench further down the hallway and Monica sat herself down beside him.

"Why did you come back to this house? Why didn't you stay on the outside?" Monica asked her patient.

"I came back because of Mina. She's sicker than me but she's very dear to me. She's a rich soul."

"Mina's an uncut gem," Monica said sadly, "but we can't save her. Her father couldn't be saved either."

"Nurse Monica, maybe my condition's no better than Mina's . . . Maybe the prognosis for me is just as sad. Tell me, Nurse; you must know."

"I only wish that Mina were as well as you; then I could believe that she could be saved. The Plasticine sculptures she makes are all unhealthy expressions of her spirit. It might be better for you, and for her, if you left this house."

"Excuse me, Nurse," Duvdivani said meekly, "but why is it that you chose such an unhappy profession? You're young and pretty; what's the good of letting your life go dark in this house? Why don't you escape from here?"

At this question, Monica stiffened. She would never have thought that a person as ill as Duvdivani would be able to see another's life so clearly. The question moved Monica deeply and she thought about how to answer her patient. "Duvdivani . . . someone has to work here. Someone has to devote her life to this place. What would you say if, one day, someone else came instead of me? You would probably right away tell Mina, 'You see, Mina-leh, Monica went away because we gave her a hard time . . .' And Dr. Asasian would say, 'Monica left her job to go study biology. What else do you expect from a girl who's still so young?'"

They stopped talking abruptly when Mina came out of a door down the hall. She was holding in her hand a little Plasticine sculpture that looked a Mesopotamian figurine.

"That's the soldier in Room 3," said Duvdivani. "Did you make that just now? Did he model for you?"

"No. His image follows me everywhere. War; war brought him here. War!" Mina angrily threw the sculpture at the door, breaking its arms, then began to sob in the silence.

Duvdivani went up to her and patted her head. "Minaleh, my darling little Mina, there won't be any more wars here in our land. I promise you!"

Mina raised her head and looked first at Duvdivani, then at Monica, asking, "Who will give me back my childhood? There, in Krakow, near the Wawel, that's where my childhood lies. My mother's in the gas chambers. My father's in the gas chambers. Who'll find my childhood?"

Duvdivani knelt beside Mina. "Me. I will, Minaleh, I'll bring it to you. Just don't be so sad. What did Dr. Asasian say to you today? Tell us."

"He said that I should go home to the kibbutz, that I should work in the garden and throw aside all this nonsense about becoming a sculptor, a musician. I asked him, 'Dr. Asasian, who'll give me back my childhood?'

"To that he answered, 'Everyone has a childhood left behind somewhere. No one gets it back.'"

"Minaleh, I'll give it back to you. Calm down. I'll go looking for it."

Mina became frightened and began to sob. "Are you going to leave me? Who will I have then? Who'll smile that dear smile for me? I don't want you to go away. Don't go. Stay. I'm so afraid of being alone."

Monica took them each by the arm and began to tell them in a cheerful voice that she had a surprise for them: tonight, she was going to give a lecture on the Jewish artist Modigliani. She'd brought thirty illustrations. Everyone would be able to ask questions.

They received this news happily. Monica led them to the table where all the patients were sitting for dinner. On the table were scattered plastic dishes. Ronit, a dark-skinned girl with two deep dimples in her cheeks, was playing a tune on a paper serviette. She kept bursting into laughter and sticking her tongue out at Duvdivani.

Lolita, a tall woman, held a notebook in her hand, continually making notes. "To my beloved Prince Theophile," she said, when asked.

Mina asked her, "Would you like me to draw a portrait of your Theophile?"

Duvdivani, patting Mina's hand, added, "My Mina is an artist!"

One by one, the patients left the dining room. One by one, each threw a parting shot at the others. Only a Jew with a long half-gray beard was left sitting at the end of the table. He was rocking and reciting Psalms and sighing. Monica let him sit there and turned out the lights, leaving only one small light by the exit.

The whole place became quiet. A strange silence lamented along with the recitation of the Psalms. A tall shadow stretched along the wall the long-bearded man was sitting beside. His beard took on strange shapes, like a half-dead cat. He sat for a long time in the semi-darkness. Then Monica came, raised him from the bench and said, "Time to go to bed. What's your name?"

The man looked at her and said, "Krakovski. I come from the Other World . . . in the Other World, no one asked me my name."

"Are there many who recite Psalms there?"

"They all disappeared from the Other World. They left me by myself. That's why I'm here. They told me I was being sent to the Garden of Eden. This must be the Garden of Eden."

Monica took the man by the arm, led him out to the garden, and sat with him on a long bench.

Rumiya and the Shofar

❧

RIKUDA POTASH

Translated by Chana Thau

RUMIYA KHALIFA THE WASHERWOMAN IS NO ORDINARY washerwoman. In her heart, another world burns and glows. She doesn't mind doing laundry for strangers; what she *does* mind is the Jewish custom in which men only are allowed to blow the shofar. Rumiya has a small metal case in which lies a shofar that belonged to her husband, who had been the king of all those who blow the shofar. When he put the shofar to his mouth, it was as though he were summoning from the Tomb of the Patriarchs each and every one of the forefathers.

Every day, early in the morning, Rumiya goes to do the laundry, for a different family each day. She does laundry only for '*Shikanaz-im*. At least *they* treat her with respect: they ask her whether she'd like some fresh bread, whether she'd like an egg, whether the butter is fresh. This shows that the '*Shikanazim* have kinder hearts.

The High Holidays are drawing near, so Rumiya takes out the shofar, polishes and looks it over carefully, then wraps it in a clean white towel and takes it with her to the 'Shikanazi lady she works for. "Khavivati," she asks shyly, "can you tell me if a woman is permitted to blow the shofar?" "No, yekirati," the lady, who is very orthodox, answers. "Women have not been granted permission by the Almighty to pray at the pulpit nor to blow the shofar. The Holy One chose women to do very different things. Women too may pray, but their prayers join with those of the men, and it is in that way that the women's prayers rise to heaven."

Burning with shame, Rumiya goes and sits on the ground, wringing out the wash with her careworn hands. But now that she has begun to talk, she will not let go of the thought. She starts over again: "Khavivati, I would like some answers from you! Don't think that my hands are capable only of doing laundry for strangers. They also are capable of many other things: they can sew and knit—and they can also hold a shofar!"

The orthodox lady, who wears a scarf to cover her head and ears, looks at Rumiya and begins to get a little uneasy. "What do you mean, Rumiya? Are you saying that you can hold a shofar in your hands? You don't mean to tell me that in *your* community, you are allowed to blow the shofar!?"

Rumiya lets her hands, wrinkled as yellow mushrooms, rest, closes her eyes, and says, "My husband died young. Of those who blow the shofar, he was the best. His shofar was one with God. My husband comes to me at night and, with his dead lips, teaches me how to blow the shofar. But how can I do it, when I am not allowed into the synagogue? Nobody minds when women huff and puff away in their daily work, but it's only the men who are allowed to blow a true blast on the shofar. I must keep my shofar because if my husband were to come to me again and see that the shofar were not there, he would be terribly upset! Should I get my dead husband all upset? He may well know that women are not supposed to blow the shofar, but still he comes to teach me!"

The orthodox lady looks at her and becomes lost in thought. "Rumiya, if you like, I can ask our rabbi. He will tell me what you should do with the shofar."

Rumiya has just finished the laundry. It is hanging on the line, waving in the wind; Rumiya is rubbing a little oil into her wrinkled hands. Her lady is already preparing some things to give Rumiya to take home: an old nightgown and a pair of misshapen shoes the lady can no longer wear. Rumiya takes the shofar from its white towel and shows it to the lady: "Have you ever in your life seen a shofar so clean and well kept? Should I, God forbid, entrust it to strange hands? I will take it with me to the grave!"

The lady is afraid to touch the shofar. Never in her whole life has she thought, or even dared to think, of blowing the shofar. It is not right that a Jewish woman should do so! She snaps angrily at Rumiya, "Listen here! Who do you think you are, wanting to blow the shofar? The prophetess Deborah? Salome? Queen Esther? Judith? Are you not ashamed to ask the Creator to let you stand and blow the shofar?" Her face is covered with white blotches of rage.

Rumiya sits on the ground, sorting through and examining the hand-me-down clothing that the lady has prepared for her to take home. Her shrewd eyes see the holes in the nightgown; they also see the stains that will not wash out. To her the most ridiculous item is the corset with its rusty hooks. She lays it against her slim body, right against her belly, and says with a smile, "My friend, this is not for me. Our foremothers, Rachel and Sarah, did not wear such things. Their bodies were slender as palm trees. Do palm trees need corsets? Give it to an Ashkenazi woman. She can dress herself up in it. We Yemenite women like our own clothing."

Then Rumiya tries on the misshapen shoes, which are too big for her. Besides, Rumiya likes to wear black lace-up shoes with heels. She has small feet she is proud of.

The lady is seething. Rumiya takes her little change purse out of her bosom and puts her wages in it. Then she wishes the lady a Happy New Year and walks proudly out, her head held high.

On the way, she meets Margalit the seamstress. Margalit is carrying over her shoulder a dress she has made for Rumiya's neighbor. Together, they walk toward Mazkeret Moshe, the little alley where Rumiya lives. The doors of her house are low, narrow, and green. In the yard is a bowl with dried watermelon seeds. Rumiya goes ahead, her steps small but steady. Margalit takes a handful of seeds.

Rumiya enters through her green doors. She locks them behind her, unpacks the shofar, looks at it again, and puts it to her lips. But she does not dare blow. She opens her metal case and carefully, as one lays a child to sleep in its carriage, she puts the shofar away.

As she eats, Rumiya thinks again about the lady who asked whether she were Mother Sarah or Mother Rachel. She laughs out loud, saying, "And who am I? Am I not of the same family?" Defiantly she adds, "And with God's help, I *will* some day blow the shofar!"

Bone tired, she falls asleep. In her sleep, her hands, shriveled from washing, turn into wings—two white wings! She dreams that the angels bring her wings so she may come to the Almighty and give him her husband's shofar.

When she awakens, she quickly slips on her wooden clogs and runs to see if the shofar is still in its case.

Glossary

❦

Adar: the sixth month in the Hebrew calendar.

Ashkenazi: Jew of Eastern European origin.

Baba: grandmother.

Bris: ritual circumcision and its accompanying ceremony, held on the eighth day of a male infant's life.

Challah: traditional egg bread eaten on the Sabbath and holidays; often braided or twisted.

Chanukah: the eight-day Feast of Lights.

Chassid: member of a Jewish mystical sect who adheres strictly to traditional customs (plural Chassidim; adjective Chassidic).

Cheder: an elementary school in which children are taught Hebrew and religion.

Cholent: a stew of beans and meat prepared overnight for the Sabbath.

Dybbuk: in Jewish folklore, a spirit that takes possession of a human being.

Gemara: part of the Talmud, a book of commentary on the Mishna.

Goye (Yiddish): feminine version of "goy"; literally "nation"; non-Jew, gentile; can be used pejoratively.

Halvah: a confection made of ground sesame seeds and honey.

Kaddish: the prayer recited by mourners after the death of a close relative.

Keynahore (Yiddish): literally "no Evil Eye"; phrase used to ward off bad luck.

Khavivati (Hebrew): "my dear"; term of polite affection.

Kiddush: the blessing said over wine or food on a holy day or the Sabbath; also the meal accompanying the blessing.

Landsman: fellow countryman.

Mamzer (Yiddish): according to Jewish law, a child born out of an incestuous relationship, adultery, or a mixed marriage, not a child born out of wedlock. The term is also more generally used for an illegitimate child, bastard. Can be used pejoratively to refer to an untrustworthy person; can also be used as a term of endearment for someone who is clever.

Mandlen (Yiddish): almonds; also almond-shaped soup nuts.

Maskil; maskilim (pl.) (Hebrew): an adherent of the Haskalah (Jewish Enlightenment).

Melamed (Yiddish): schoolteacher.

Oy: expletive; oh.

Rebele (Yiddish): little rabbi; diminutive of *rebe.*

Schlemiel: gullible, inept person; fool.

Shabbes: the Jewish Sabbath, which starts at sunset Friday and ends at sunset Saturday.

Shammes: the sexton of a synagogue.

Shavuot: the spring holiday which commemorates the giving of the law at Mount Sinai.

'Shikanazi; 'Shikanazim (pl.) (Hebrew): slang for Ashkenazi Jews used by Sephardic Jews.

Shiva: the traditional seven-day mourning period for the dead.

Shofar: the ram's horn trumpet used in synagogues during the High Holidays of Rosh Hashanah and Yom Kippur.

Shoykhet (Yiddish): ritual butcher who ensures that animals are slaughtered according to Jewish law and are therefore kosher.

Shtetl: a small town or village with a Jewish population.

Tanach: the Jewish scriptures including the Torah, the Prophets and the Writings.

Tateshe (Yiddish): diminutive of *tate,* father.

Tefillin: the phylacteries, two small leather cases containing scripture texts traditionally worn during morning prayer.

Tisha b'Av: fast day commemorating the destruction of the temple at Jerusalem.

Tselem elokhim (Hebrew): image of God.

Vey iz mir (Yiddish): woe is me.

Yekirati (Hebrew): "my dear"; term of polite affection.

Yeshiva: school for higher religious instruction.

Yom Kippur: solemn fast day during the High Holidays; the Day of Atonement.

Zaida: grandfather.

Zogerin (Yiddish): female prayer leader.

Bibliographical Information

❦

Bercovitch, Bryna. "Becoming Revolutionary." Compiled from Bercovitch's weekly column in *Der kanader adler* [The Canadian Eagle] on the following dates: December 18, 1945; May 9, 1948; June 2, 1948; January 14, 1949; December 21, 1949; April 25, 1950; May 10, 1950; June 4, 1950; August 31, 1950.

Broches, Rochel. "Little Abrahams" *[Avremelekh].* In *Shpinen* [Spinners] (Minsk: A. G. Stalig, 1940) pages 14–31.

Frankel-Zaltzman, Paula (Pesia). "A Natural Death." Excerpted from *Heftling # 94771: iberlebenishn in Daytshe lagern* [Prisoner #94771: Experiences in a German Camp] (Montreal: Montreal Latvian Mutual Aid Association, 1949). The original translation of *Heftling #94771* was published on the Internet as Volume 28 (ISBN 0-88947-406-0) of the Memoirs of Holocaust Survivors in Canada series, by the Concordia University Chair in Canadian Jewish Studies; Mervin Butovsky and Kurt Jonassohn, Series Editors; Karin Björnson, Assistant Editor; Montreal Institute for Genocide and Human Rights Studies and Concordia University Chair in Canadian Jewish Studies.

Halpern, Frume. "Goodbye, Honey," "Blessed Hands," *[Gebentshte hent]* and "Three Meetings" *[Drei mol bagegnt].* In *Gebentshte hent* [Blessed Hands] (New York: Yiddisher Kultur Farband, Inc.[Ykuf], 1963) pages 178–188, 9–13 and 65–70.

Hamer-Jacklyn, Sarah. "A Love Story" *[A libe].* In *Shtot un shtetl* [City and Town] (Tel Aviv: I. L. Peretz Publishing House, 1964) pages 175–182. "A Guest" *[A gast].* In *Lebns un geshtaltn: dertseylungen* [Lives and Portraits: Stories] (New York: The Novoradomsker Society, 1946) pages 64–78. "No More Rabbi!" *[Oys rebe].* In *Shtamen un tsvaygn: dertseylungen* [Stumps and Branches: Stories] (New York: Promotion Press,1954) pages 45–54.

Lee, Malka. "The Apple of Her Eye" *[Shvartzepel]*. In *Mayselekh far Yoselen* [Short Stories for Joseph] (Tel Aviv: I. L. Peretz Publishing House, 1969) pages 58–62.

Potash, Rikuda. "Rumiya and the Shofar" *[Rumiya un der shoyfer]* and "The Sad House in Talbiye" *[Dos troyerike hoyz in Talbiye]*. In *In geslekh fun Yerushalayim: dertseylungen* [In the Alleys of Jerusalem: Stories] (Tel Aviv: Publishing House Israel-Book, 1968) pages 129–132 and 151–156.

Rosenfarb, Chava. "Letters to God" *[Briv tsu got]*. *Di goldene keyt* [The Golden Chain], Volume 140 (1995), pages 51–72.

Viderman, Anne. "A Fiddle." A combination of *"Der aynzamer kinstler"* [The Lonesome Artist] and *"Gvald, der redakter geyt"* [Help, the Editor is Coming]. In *Umetiker shmeykhel* [Sad Smiles] (Montreal: The Northern Printing and Stationer, 1946) pages 39–42 and 186–187.

Bibliographical Information in Yiddish

AUTHOR NAMES, STORY, JOURNAL AND BOOK TITLES

✎

Bercovitch, Bryna.
Der kanader adler.

בערקאָוויטש, ברײַנע.
דער קאַנאדער אדלער.

Broches, Rochel.
Avremelekh.
Shpinen.

בראָכעס, ראחל.
אווורעמעלעכ.
שפּינען.

Frankel, Zaltzman, Paula (Pesia).
Heftling #94771: iberlebenishn in daytshe lagern.

פֿריינקל-זאַלצמאַן, פּעסיע.
העפֿטלינג נומער 94771 :
איבערלעבענישן אין דײַטשע לאַגערן.

Halpern, Frume.
Drei mol bagegnt.
Good-Bye, Honey.
Gebentshte hent.

האלפערן, פרומע.

דריי מאל באגעגנט.

גוד באי האני.

געבענטשטע הענט.

Hamer-Jacklyn, Sarah.
A gast.
Lebns un geshtaltn: dertseylungen.
Oys rebe.
Shtamen un tsvaygn: dertseylungen.
A libe.
Shtot un shtetl.

האמער-דזשאקלין, שרה.

א גאסט.

לעבנס און געשטאלטן : דערצייילונגען.

אויס רבי.

שטאמען און צוויינג : דערצייילונגען.

א ליבע.

שטאט און שטעטל.

Lee, Malka.
Shvartzepel.
Mayselekh far Yoselen.

לי, מלכה.

שווארצאפל.

מעשהלעך פאר יאסעלען.

Potash, Rikuda.
Rumiya un der shoyfer.
Dos troyerke hoyz in Talbiye.
In geslekh fun Yerushalayim: dertseylungen.

פאטאש, ריקודה.
רומיה און דער שופר.
דאס טרויעריקע הויז אין תלביה.
אין געסלער פון ירושלים : דערצייילונגען.

Rosenfarb, Chava.
Briv tsu got.
Di goldene keyt.

ראזענפעארב, חוה.
בריוו צו גאט.
די גאלדענע קייט.

Viderman, Anne.
Der aynzamer kinstler.
Gvald, der redakter geyt.
Umetiker shmeykhel.

ווידערמאן, חנה.
דער איינזאמער קינסטלער.
גוואלד דער רעדאקטאר געהט.
אומעטיקער שמייכל.

About the Translators

৯১

Sylvia Ary is a well-known Montreal artist. She has exhibited in cities across Canada as well as in the United States of America, Israel, and Mexico, and in London and Paris. She is also an illustrator; her illustrations of poems by Itzik Manger are in the Jewish Public Library in Montreal, and her illustrations of stories by Isaac Bashevis Singer are in the Museum of the University of Texas in Austin.

Miriam Beckerman's translations from Yiddish have appeared in *Pakn Treger* [Book Pedlar] and *Parchment.* She has also translated from English to Yiddish for the *Forward* and *Canadian Jewish News.* She has been translator for a number of books, including *Wartime Experiences in Lithuania,* part of the Library of Holocaust Testimonies (eds. Lozansky-Bogomolnaya and Logan), and Konrad Charmatz's *Nightmares: Memoirs of the Years of Horror Under Nazi Rule in Europe, 1939–1945,* as well as *A Thousand Threads, a Story Told Through Yiddish Letters* (eds. and co-translators Lily Poritz Miller and Olga Zabludoff).

Sacvan Bercovitch is Powell M. Cabot Research Professor of American Literature at Harvard University. He received his B.A. from Concordia University in Montreal (where he grew up). A Fellow of the American Academy of Arts and Sciences and former President of the American Studies Association, he has lectured and published widely on American literature and culture. He has also translated various Yiddish writers, including Sholem Aleichem and Canadian author Isaac Zipper.

Luba Cates is a first-generation Canadian. Yiddish was her first language and the only mutual tongue with her grandfather. Her parents' home was filled with Yiddish books and publications. The Winnipeg Yiddish Women Writers Reading Circle rekindled her love of the language and literature. She feels privileged to have been able to work on this translation project.

As the child of immigrant parents, **Esther Leven** spoke Yiddish in her home in Winnipeg for many years. She studied English at the University of Winnipeg and started her translating career working for the Jewish Historical Society of Western Canada (presently called the Jewish Heritage Center) in Winnipeg. For several years she wrote the column "Looking Backward" for the *Jewish Post and News* in which she translated excerpts dating from the early 1920s to the 1940s which had been published in *The Israelite Press*, a Winnipeg Yiddish newspaper.

Goldie Morgentaler is Associate Professor of English at the University of Lethbridge, where she teaches nineteenth-century British and American literature. She has published numerous translations from Yiddish to English, including several stories by I. L. Peretz. She has also translated Michel Tremblay's play *Les Belles Soeurs* from French into Yiddish. Morgentaler is the translator of much of Chava Rosenfarb's work, including *The Tree of Life* and *Survivors: Seven Short Stories,* for which Morgentaler won the 2005 Helen and Stan Vine Jewish Book Award.

Arnice Pollock was born and has lived all her life in Winnipeg. She is a graduate of the I. L. Peretz Folk School and holds a B.A. and B.Ed. from the University of Manitoba. She taught at the Peretz School in the Judaic and General Studies programs. She has also translated Shimshon Heilik's Yiddish novel *Conflict Between Two Worlds.*

Chana Thau, born and bred in Winnipeg after the Second World War, spoke Yiddish first. She worked for many years as a French-English translator for the Federal government. Thau has edited *Seasons of Our Lives,* an anthology of life writing, and is currently working as a personal historian, helping individuals to write their life stories.

Roz Usiskin has an M.A. in Sociology and an Honors B.A. in History. She taught Sociology at the University of Winnipeg and was the Executive Director of the Manitoba Multicultural Resource Center. Usiskin served as President of the Jewish Historical Society of Western Canada and the Jewish Heritage Center of Western Canada. She has published a number of scholarly articles, including "The Winnipeg Jewish Community: Its Radical Elements 1905–1918" *(Historical and Scientific Society of Manitoba Transactions,* Series III, No.33, 1976–7) and "Winnipeg's Jewish Women of the Left: Radical and Traditional" *(Jewish Life and Times,* Vol. VIII, 2003).

Permissions

❧